D1616952

Books by Rick Sowash

The Boy Who Would Be Famous
> The Comic Endeavors and Curious Pursuits of
> an Adventurous Lad Growing Up in America's Heartland

Ripsnorting Whoppers
> A Book of Ohio Tall Tales

Heroes of Ohio
> 23 True Tales of Courage and Character

Critters, Flitters and Spitters
> 24 Amazing Ohio Animal Tales

The Cabin Down the Glen (by Odell Shepard: discovered, edited and
> published by Rick Sowash)

What Book Next?
> Practical and Inspiring Insights for Readers

Was That Your Piece?
> A Salmagundi of Humor

For more information visit www.sowash.com

THE BLUE ROCK

BY RICK SOWASH

Rick Sowash Publishing Company
6836 School Street
Cincinnati OH 45244
www.sowash.com

Cover Design: Randall Wright
Interior Design: Pat Marriott

Printed in the United States of America

Publisher's Cataloging-in-Information Data
Sowash, Rick, 1950-
The Blue Rock
September 2021

ISBN: 9798490518648
Independently Published

1. Humor

The Cover

Just so you know, the blue rock pictured
on the cover of this book
is the actual Blue Rock.

– The Author

Photo credit: Randall Wright

The most beautiful thing we can experience is the mysterious.
It is the source of all true art and all science.
— *Albert Einstein*

"On the contrary, Watson, it is of the greatest importance,"
Holmes avowed, "because it is inexplicable."
— *Arthur Conan Doyle*

Credo quia absurdum.
(Translated by some: I believe because it is absurd.)
(Translated by others: It is certain because it is impossible.)
— *Often misattributed to Tertullian*

From stones and poets you may know,
Nothing more active is than that which least seems so.
— *Francis Thompson*

Contents

Introduction

WRITERS WRITE FOR MANY REASONS: to earn money, to achieve fame, to gain credibility, to argue a point.

I wrote this book purely for the fun of it. I wrote it for you, for my friends. My motivation was the hope of entertaining you, of causing you to smile and maybe even chuckle as you read it.

We are living in a grim time. Climate change, poverty, COVID, white supremacy groups, military folly, rising autocracies, wobbling democracies – these and a dozen other egregious issues crowd in upon me as I sit in the quiet of my garden.

I wish these things need not have happened in my time.

"So do all who live to see such times," said Gandalf. "But that is not for them to decide. All we have to do is to decide what to do with the time that is given us."

What to do? Call the elected officials who represent me? I do that, usually a couple times a week. Vote? Of course. Stay informed? Yep. I read the news every day, even though much of it depresses me.

But what else? None of those activities lead to radiant serenity; they don't even help me move happily through the day.

Pray? Worship? Affirm what is good? Assure my loved ones that they are loved? Keep in touch with friends? Try to be of some use to someone else? Share my gifts, such as they are, with the world, such as it is?

Write another book in the hope that it will entertain my friends?

Yes! All of the above! I'll give a few folks a new book to discover. The mere act of putting a new book in peoples' hands is a brief moment of escape from all that is grim.

I asked myself, what shall this new book be about? The answer has lain within reach for almost a half century: my Blue Rock. The idea grew from a conversation with a friend.

When I shared the story of my discovery of "The Blue Rock" with my friend the Rev. Rebekah Nolt, the idea emerged that I ought to share the story, too, with our congregation at Mt. Auburn Presbyterian Church, perhaps as a children's sermon. I set out to write such a sermon. I would make it short and intriguing. It quickly become too long. I kept the long version but cut it down ruthlessly to a shorter version for use in church.

Then I realized that the larger version could make the first chapter of a book. I sent it to my old friend and mentor, Dick Figge, and he replied:

> Surely you are blessed with a circle of highly intelligent, creative, and imaginative friends. I like to think of your showing them the rock, then settling in your garden pavilion during the cocktail hour. And in that glowing hour, when valor is

reborn and spirits expand, they offer you their own explanations of the provenance of the Blue Rock. This could be the frame for a collection of fantastic stories, each narrator a memorably distinct and colorful character with his or her own vision of this odd and event-filled world.

(He writes so well, doesn't he? His prose is inspiring.)

Inspired and encouraged by Dick's idea, I happily set to work.

Before you read it, please let me explain a few things.

All the friends who tell me their theories about "The Blue Rock" in this book are real people, though with two exceptions I have given them fictional names. The exceptions are my old friend Dick "Grippy" Ferrell and the late Walt Landgraf. Walt was a wonderful man and a great help to me when I published Odell Shepard's *The Cabin Down the Glen*, one of the most meaningful endeavors of my career. I wanted to pay homage to Walt; disguising his name would have been a missed opportunity.

As for the others, since I put words in their mouths, I thought it best to veil their identities. I didn't want to embarrass them. Or, for that matter, to embarrass myself. Reading my account, they might protest, "I would never express it that way," or raise objections I could not foresee.

In some cases, the disguise is very thin. Everyone at my church will recognize Chris Miller; he is named Biff Triller in the book. I am not worried. Chris is a close friend and almost impossible to offend.

The book recounts quite a few historical incidents or true anecdotes from my own experiences. For instance, I have ascended in a hot air balloon. The account of that experience is accurate, though in the book I am not the one telling the story.

Some of the more wildly improbable details are true. Mozart's librettist actually did briefly manage a general store in Sunbury, Pennsylvania. Daniel Boone really was at Braddock's Defeat as a wagon driver. The first dental school in America truly was in Bainbridge, Ohio. For well over a century, the colony of Connecticut, unique among the coastal colonies, literally did once extend 3,000 miles west to the Pacific Ocean. Bogart and Bacall certainly did marry and honeymoon at Malabar Farm in Richland County, Ohio.

So part of the fun of reading this book will be trying to discern which assertions are factual and which are invented. I intentionally tried to blur the separation of fiction and non-fiction, passing it all off as "true," and trusting my friends to take it all with however many grains of salt they choose.

On the other hand, I'll confess right now that the Serpent Mound seems never to have had an eye (more's the pity), and the Vikings did not, so far as I know, mark the extent of their conquests with a blue rock, credible as these assertions might seem.

I drew the line at the supernatural. Unlike some folks, I am not interested in Bigfoot. Same with ancient alien landings and ghost-sightings. Many enjoy contemplating such things, and I say "more power to 'em." The paranormal had no place in this book. A good story can be fabricated from believable material.

The more credible a story is, the more powerful will be its narrative tug.

A second purpose I had in writing this book was to present Ohio, specifically north-central Ohio, as a land with a rich history, peopled with colorful figures who live through exciting adventures. A storied land, a fabled land. Most of my books attempt to explore and express the character of Ohio, its unique identity, its people, its places, and its past.

I remember my daughter, when she was little, asking why we didn't live "somewhere cool." I asked her where that would be. California, Hawaii. I remember feeling that way, too, when I was an adolescent. It seemed to me that just about anywhere else had more personality, character, interest, history, depth, culture, what have you, than boring, clunky, cautious Ohio.

I still feel that way to some extent. I've written books and even music "about" Ohio as my small part to enrich the cultural loam.

I love to think that someone, after reading this book, might say, "I had no idea north-central Ohio was such a fascinating place!"

In short, it's all part of my long effort to make my own cultural environment sufficiently nourishing for me to thrive in. My way of living "somewhere cool" has been to try my best to bloom where I was planted. In Scouts, we used to say, "If it's not fun, make it fun." That's what I've tried to do for Ohio.

Lastly, I wish to express my gratitude to the following friends: the Rev. Rebekah Nolt for sparking the idea for this book; Dick Figge for his encouragement and suggestion for a framework for the stories; Julie Malkin, Terry Burch, Phil Lichtenstein, and Chris Miller for sharing their theories of the provenance of the Blue Rock; Pat Marriott for editing the manuscript so skillfully; and Randy Wright for designing the covers. And many thanks to my dear wife Jo, who copy-edited and proofread the final draft with exquisite care.

To all of you, I want to say what the grateful Sebastian says to his friend Antonio in *Twelfth Night*:

> I can no other answer make but thanks,
> and thanks, and ever thanks.

Rick Sowash
Cincinnati OH
September 2021

1

The Blue Rock

THERE WAS A MAN who lived in a village near a dark forest.

I am that man. This story is true.

The village was Bellville. It lies, drowsily, in southern Richland County in north-central Ohio. Around it are farms, fields, and forests.

My wife Jo and I lived in Bellville for the first twelve years of our married life. We founded and operated a bed and breakfast country inn there, the Frederick Fitting House. When our children were born in the Mansfield General Hospital, ten miles north, it was to Bellville that we brought them home.

The inn offered a library with floor-to-ceiling bookshelves. I ordered a map of Jefferson Township, of which Bellville is the center, from the U.S. Geological Survey. I had it framed and hung on the library wall. It displayed rivers and streams in tiny threads of blue ink, houses and buildings in minuscule squares of black, and the area's forests in large, irregular rectangles, triangles, and trapezoids of pale green.

I adore maps. They are the fruit of the union of mathematics and geography. Map reading stimulates both memory and anticipation.

In studying the map, I located the region's largest forest and its midpoint that lay farthest from any road. Standing there, I would be as far away from a road as it was possible to get in southern Richland County. I resolved to go to that place.

It took some doing. I parked my car in the ferns along the unpaved township road at the edge of the forest. I carefully maneuvered around and past the poison ivy and bushwhacked through the honeysuckle and the thorny multi-floral rose bushes that thrive on the edges of the woods of Richland County.

Leaving those behind, I entered the forest proper. There is almost no primeval forest left in north-central Ohio. The pioneers cut it down, clearing the land for farming. But this was a healthy, second-growth forest with many large, old trees. Maple, beech, oak, hickory. The occasional walnut.

Aside from a few aimless deer paths, the forest was trackless, and the lay of the land was rough and uneven. North-central Ohio is known for its watercourses, and I had to cross several small creeks and streams, scrambling down into and up out of ravines, large and small. I didn't know exactly where I was, but after an hour I figured I was about three-tenths of a mile from the road. I was pretty close to the center of the forest.

And there I came upon something surprising and mysterious, something that made me wonder. A blue rock.

It was about two feet in width and height, its surface alternately smooth and rough. I supposed it weighed a hundred pounds. It had small holes, a dozen or so, randomly placed and of various radii and depths, seemingly drilled into its surface. Its color was breathtakingly beautiful; in vivid contrast to the surrounding Kelly green of fern fronds and leaves, the gray-lavender tree trunks, and the burnt-brown leaf mold thickly covering the forest floor, the rock presented a bright, almost turquoise blue, the blue of a summer sky, with artful streaks and striations of a milky, cloud-like white. It might have passed for an enormous and imaginative dessert: a little vanilla ice cream marbleized into a blueberry sorbet.

How did it get there?

The rocks of Richland County were left by retreating glaciers at the end of the last Ice Age. Not this rock. I know southern Richland County. I grew up in Richland County and lived there for more than 40 years. I know the glens, creeks, rock formations, moraines, even a few shallow caves. This was unlike any rock I had ever seen in Richland County or anywhere else. I thought of the gemology exhibition at the Museum of Natural History in New York City. Stunning things are to be seen there, but nothing exactly like this.

If glaciers didn't leave the rock, then how did it get there? Transporting it to that location from the nearest road would have been a daunting task. I could lift it, I found, but only just barely. I could not have carried it, staggering, farther than a few yards.

If someone had undertaken the considerable challenge of conveying it from the road to set it down just there, then why?

Why go to the trouble of placing this beautiful blue rock so deep in a dark, pathless, seldom-visited forest?

Perhaps someone dropped it from the sky. But why lug such a heavy thing onto an airplane only to push it out the door? Why drop it from a hot air balloon? And why at the precise moment needed to land it, middlemost, in the most heavily forested and least populated part of north-central Ohio?

Was there some crime involved? Was it a telltale piece of evidence ditched by a criminal who intended to retrieve it but then failed to do so for reasons that can only be surmised?

Did surveyors put it there to indicate a boundary? Why use a strange blue rock for that purpose instead of a stake or a fence post flagged with a bright-colored rag?

Did it mark the site of a tomb or a buried treasure? Was it a shrine?

Had it descended from outer space? I've seen meteorites in natural history museums; that it was not. Objects from space melt, even vaporize, from the friction caused by their passing through the atmosphere. This rock showed no signs of melting. It couldn't have drifted at leisure through the atmosphere. What rock plummets slowly?

Was it left there three centuries ago by the Shawnee or the Delaware? Or ten centuries ago by the Mound Builders? Placing of such a thing in such a place would transmit a clear message: "We were here."

Almost everything has an explanation. We know all about the objects that daily surround us, go where we will. And if we don't know, we never doubt that somebody somewhere knows what they are, where they come from, what their purpose is, and how they came to be located where they are.

Not this blue rock. Surely, it had a story. But who could tell it?

"Some things that should not have been forgotten were lost. History became legend, legend became myth, and it passed out of all knowledge ... until, when chance came, it was discovered anew by the most unlikely creature imaginable ...": a composer wandering afoot in the deep woods of north-central Ohio.

Thus began a new chapter in its curious history. No longer would this object be merely "a blue rock." It had gained a name. It had become "The Blue Rock." What a difference a few capital letters make!

Now named, the Blue Rock became restless. Upon my discovery – or rediscovery – of it, it resumed its migration, its pilgrimage, its trek.

I had to possess it.

I hornswoggled the skeptical Dick "Grippy" Ferrell, my friend since our Boy Scouting days, into helping me fetch it. On the phone, enlisting his aid, I described it to him as best I could.

"Bullshit," he said.

That was not very nice. Grippy rarely employed vulgarities. A bit taken aback, I chided him by reciting the eleventh Scout Law:

"A Scout is Clean," I said. "That doesn't only mean that you wash your hands and bathe. It also applies to the way you talk." He knew I was razzing him.

"I meant it literally," he explained. "It's obviously a cow pie."

"A cow pie? It's sky blue and hard as a rock."

"So you have said, Sodie. It's clearly a petrified cow pie."

"I don't think so. What species of bovine excretes bright blue manure?"

"Easy. It was plopped there by none other than Babe, Paul Bunyan's celebrated Blue Ox. That's why it's blue."

He had me there.

"Look, wise guy, are you going to help me or not?"

"Of course, I'll help you."

We returned to the woods together, bringing a quantity of rope and a sturdy two-wheeled dolly of the sort used by strong men delivering cases of beer.

As we made our way through the lush and fronded wealth of a northeastern American forest in early summer, I wondered if I could find the rock again. As I'd made my way back to my car after finding it, I had made special note of where it lay and had been very alert to helpful landmarks. A fallen tree here, a boulder there, a clearing, a glen.

Would it still be there? Might it have somehow moved of its own volition like the mysterious "sailing stones" of Death Valley? The very existence and location of the Blue Rock were already highly unlikely, and I had begun to think that anything was possible.

It was still there. Grippy was impressed. "Still think it's a petrified cow pie?" I asked. He did not reply. We set to work, lashing the rock to the hand cart, wrapping and frapping the rope as we'd learned to do in Scouts.

Carting it through the woods and back to the car was a devil of a job, demanding sweat and strain and the greater part of a June afternoon.

Oomphing it up into the trunk of my car required the combined strength of we two big strong men. Under its weight, the car's rear end sagged low; I drove slowly for fear of scraping the underside of my vehicle on the pot-holed gravel roads.

At length, we placed it among the day lilies in the backyard of the Sowash home in Bellville.

When we relocated to Gambier some years later, and then again to Cincinnati six years after that, the baffled movers who had to lug the Blue Rock aboard the moving van asked me, "What is this?"

I replied truthfully: "I don't know."

Two and a half years ago, our son, Chapman Sowash, helped us move it yet again from our downtown apartment where we had lived for fourteen years to what will most likely be our last home, a country property near Mariemont.

For now, the rock graces our garden. It reposes in the symmetrical place of honor – at the far end of the straight line one could make by coming down our front walk, passing through the bright red front door, on through the foyer, the family room, the master bedroom, and out through the French doors to the backyard garden, through the Greek Revival pavilion, on through the fountain (so to speak), and ending at the far extreme of the property, right up against the forest green picket fence. Symmetrical, see?

It rests, yes, but it is restive, its spirit unquiet. The Blue Rock and I both know that my stewardship is temporary. In five, ten, or fifteen years, Jo and I will be no more. When, sooner or later, our home and all the treasures within it are dispersed, the rock will move again. Who can say where?

What does the Blue Rock want? It wants what all the elements of Creation want, large and small, near and distant: to fulfill its destiny. But what is its destiny, its destination?

I've been an admiring reader of Tolkien for sixty years. Seven times have I read *The Lord of the Rings*, including once, aloud, to my 7-year-old son – one of the greatest experiences of my life and his. We still remember it fondly. Tolkien makes me wonder: does the Blue Rock confer traits, talents, or powers of imagination upon its custodian? Have changes entered my life as the result of my possession of it?

The Blue Rock is utterly baffling. It cannot be understood or explained. In this way, it is like the Mind of God. That is why I revere it, why I have carried it with us from home to home for nearly half a century, why I have positioned it in a place of honor.

It is a monument. It memorializes no soldier, known or unknown, no leader, famous or forgotten, no esteemed ancestor, no beloved pet. It commemorates no known event. It metaphorizes no virtue, not courage, honor, loyalty, or justice. There are many monuments to such people, events, and virtues, and we appreciate them. The Blue Rock honors something rarer.

It is a monument to The Inexplicable, a monument to All That Is and Always Will Be Beyond Knowing, a monument to an inarguable assertion: There Are Things We Will Never Understand.

The Blue Rock is worthy of reverence because it emblemizes a way of thinking about The Unknowable.

It communicates so much and so little, saying only: "Abide."

The Blue Rock excites wonder in the hearts; it prompts theories in the minds of all who hear of my discovery and of my communion with it during this one short chapter of its long and mysterious history.

2

Serpent Mound

LUCAS PENDLETON IS A scholar, deeply informed about all manner of matters pertaining to the history of architecture. Now retired, he was formerly a Full Professor of Architecture at the University of Cincinnati and the author of many distinguished scholarly articles. His wife Melinda is an artist.

After sharing dinner at our home one evening, we and the Pendletons adjourned to the pavilion in the center of our upper garden. Lucas immediately admired the pavilion we built, reminiscent of a small Greek temple in keeping with the Greek Revival style of our 1830 home.

While Melinda and Jo made their way through the upper and lower gardens, talking bird-lore and flower-lore, Lucas and I settled ourselves in the rocking chairs in the pavilion to indulge in a "feast of reason and flow of soul."

I told Lucas the story of my discovery of the Blue Rock, and of my subsequent puzzlement.

He listened with close attention, his blue-grey eyes staring through his large, black-framed spectacles, balanced on his angular beak of a nose. Briefly, Holmes would have known him for the intelligent, creative and imaginative scholar he is, possessed of a keen wit and a lively fancy. The tilt of his head as he listened, plainly showed him to be a man who had searched for unicorns, even if only in libraries. A light breeze occasionally fluttered through his white-streaked mane of long, grayish hair.

At length, having recounted the story of the Blue Rock, I escorted him to the rear of the lower garden and showed him the thing itself.

He stared at it in silence, shaking his large head with wonder.

"Oh, my Lord in Heaven," he said at long last. "Do you know what you have here? You have found and now possess the long-lost eye of the Serpent Mound."

We returned to the rocking chairs in the pavilion whereupon Lucas commenced a lecture on the subject nearest and dearest to his heart, the ancient earthworks of Ohio.

"The earliest accounts of the Serpent Mound," he began, "which date from the 1700s, make mention of the eye of the Serpent, describing it as a dazzling stone, teal-blue in color. Oral tradition has it that the stone was discovered in Peru on the mountain slopes near the fabled Machu Picchu. The ancient Mound Builders are known to have traded flint from Ohio quarries with many other First Nations peoples, as far away as the Pacific Northwest, the Florida Everglades, the ancient cliff dwellings of the Southwest, and even as far away as Peru and Chile.

"No one knows or can guess how long the Peruvian forebears of the once mighty Inca empire possessed the stone, but their need for the flint from which they fashioned arrowheads, spearheads, knives and axes superseded their attachment to the stone, and it was bargained away.

"The rock that became the eye of the Serpent was transported from the mountains of Peru through the jungles of Mayan Central America, across the plains of the region known to us as Texas, to the banks of the Mississippi, floated on a raft and towed by canoes upstream to the Ohio, and finally up Brush Creek to a point very near the plateau on which is built the Serpent Mound. From there, the local natives carried it up the steep slopes of the plateau, probably singing in a heightened state of religious exultation, and finally to the Serpent Mound, positioning it as the eye in the Serpent's head, ceremonially gifting the creature with sight.

"Like many of Ohio's ancient earthworks, including some that the pioneers later plowed under, the Serpent Mound was first surveyed and described by Ephraim Squier and Edwin Davis. They recorded their research in their book *Ancient Monuments of the Mississippi Valley*, published in 1848 and one of the most important books in American architectural history. This book, so crucial to what we know of the ancient earthworks of Ohio, was the first publication of the then newly-formed Smithsonian Institution.

"Despite describing the Serpent Mound in great detail, even including a topographical map to illustrate its exact shape and size, Squier and Davis made no mention of the blue rock that had been placed as the Serpent's eye. If it was still there when they surveyed it, they would surely have called attention to it.

"The Mound was purchased in 1887 by Professor Frederick W. Putnam for the Peabody Museum, making it the first privately funded archaeological preserve in the United States. Between 1886 and 1889 Putnam excavated and restored it as well as other nearby mounds. The Serpent had clearly had an eye, but his search for it yielded no result.

"The Serpent Mound plateau and some of the surrounding acres were later donated to the Ohio Archaeological and Historical Society. Through the Society's efforts the site later became a state park.

"There is an ovoid mound within what appear to be the Serpent's jaws. Some researchers have opined that the small mound indicates a frog, or a frog laying an egg as it flees from the devouring snake. Others have deduced that the frog and egg are actually a single object, namely the head of the snake.

"Today's most frequently accepted theory is that the mound depicts a snake in the process of swallowing an egg-shaped object. This would appear to align with what we know or can guess of the cosmogony of the ancient Native Americans, in particular their widely shared notion that a giant serpent alternately and everlastingly swallowed and emitted the sun, thus explaining night and day. The serpent is depicted as it would appear either when swallowing the egg-sun at dusk or emitting it at dawn.

"In 2008, the Serpent Mound and eight other Ohio earthworks were selected by the Department of the Interior for inclusion on the United States' tentative list of sites to be submitted to UNESCO to be included on the World Heritage

List. No more prestigious honor could be conferred. If it eventually attains the World Heritage List, the Serpent Mound will take its place among the wonders of the world that include the Pyramids of Egypt, the Great Wall of China, Pompeii, Stonehenge, and the Taj Mahal.

"Aside from swallowing and emitting the sun, the mound has additional astronomical significance. For instance, if one were to stand on the tip of the Serpent's tail and look across its open jaws a tenth of a mile away – where the eye once was – one would see the North Star directly ahead. It's unlikely this happened by chance. Some astroarchaeologists have also observed what appears to be lunar significance in the curves of the snake, and also the azimuth of sunrise on the days of solstice. If that weren't enough, the shape of the mound also closely corresponds with the shape of the constellation Draco that lies between the Big and Little Dippers.

"No researcher, from Squier and Davis to the present day, has accounted for the Serpent's missing eye. It is likely that there was an eye, but after the end of the first quarter of the nineteenth century, the accounts left in letters and diaries by people who visited the mound make no mention of the blue eye-rock that had so impressed earlier visitors. It seems to have disappeared. Archaeologists have sought for it ever since but without success.

"And you may have found it! Why do I say this?

"Why indeed?" I said. "Don't ask yourself rhetorical questions. Do I ask myself rhetorical questions? No. Do I appreciate it when others ask themselves rhetorical questions? I do not. Do I wish you would get on with your fascinating tale? Absolutely. Pray, continue."

Lucas laughed and, following my orders, continued dutifully.

"Two reasons. First, if the astronomical explanation for the building of the Serpent is to be credited, then the effigy must have had an eye.

"Second, the Erie Canal opened in 1825.

"Let me explain the connection between these two seemingly disparate facts."

"Thank you for not asking yourself if you should explain the connection."

He laughed again.

(I was seeing my friend, for the first time, in his role as a celebrated lecturer at the University of Cincinnati. A gifted purveyor of facts and ideas, he had, in his long career, held the rapt attention of thousands of students, breathless and spellbound. He was the "prof" in whose course of study every student wished to enroll. He was the inspiring teacher that the students' indulgent parents, sending them off to college at great expense, hoped their children would encounter.)

"Let us imagine the Ohio woodlands on a plateau above Brush Creek a thousand years ago. Let us imagine, as vividly as we can, what was happening there at that time.

A young man digs into the forest floor. The damp, cool smell of the earth rises to his face. He digs with a large clam

15

shell and pushes the dirt into a basket. After filling it, he hoists the basket onto his shoulder. He wears a loincloth and moccasins. He is reddish-brown as a penny and glistening with sweat. It's hot work.

"He carries his basket of dirt along a path where others, doing the same, process ahead and behind him. Another line moves alongside them, going in the opposite direction with empty baskets to be filled and returned.

"As they walk, they sing a solemn song in a language that no one knows today. They sing of the great spirits they worship and especially of the Great Snake. It is for this deity that they fill, carry, and empty these baskets of dirt.

"At the end of the path a mound of fresh dirt gradually rises. The young man empties his basket and turns to go back and fill it again. He does not do this under compulsion. Like the medieval villagers who built the great cathedrals of Europe, he is motivated by his peoples' system of beliefs and mysteries.

"Why build a mound in the shape of a giant snake? The young man knew exactly why. If we could have tapped any of those people on the shoulder and asked them why they did what they were doing, they would have answered very precisely. They all believed that it was the greatest and most important thing they had ever done.

"But of course they are long gone. They left no written record.

"Nevertheless, there are clues. The most important clue is that the Serpent seems to have been built during or close to the year 1066. To us, that year is remembered for the Battle of

Hastings when William the Conqueror and his army crossed the English Channel in October and defeated the Anglo-Saxons.

"But something else happened earlier that same year that was observed all over the world. The ancient peoples of Ohio surely saw it because like all people of all time, they must have loved to watch the stars.

"One night, in the spring of 1066, they saw a change in the sky. They saw something new, something no one remembered having seen before. A new star? There it was again the next night, a little brighter. Each night it grew bigger. Watchers of the night sky everywhere were excited, confused, and fearful. Was it a good omen or a sign of coming disaster?

"Then the new star began to grow a tail. Soon it outshone all the other stars. All over the world, the star was watched in wonder and terror, the viewers likely dreading it and hoping it would shrink. But it grew steadily brighter.

"You've probably guessed what they saw. It was what we call Halley's Comet, which appeared in April 1066, and which, among other things, gave evidence to William of Normandy of God's blessing on his claim to the English throne.

"To the primitive people of ancient America, it may well have been understood to be the Great Snake of lore. It was traveling toward them, and it was probably hungry. It would eat them and everything they knew – the river, the forests, the world. They pondered what could be done to stop it.

"The wisest among them counseled: 'Build a giant snake here on the earth. When the Great Snake looks down and sees this giant snake, he will see that we honor him, that we honor the stars and the sun and the turnings of the seasons and the coming and going of the sun and the waxing and waning of the moon. Build the snake from dirt and place an eye in its head so that it can gaze back up at the Great Snake in the sky and give assurance that it is worshipped and that all is well.'

"And thus was built the Serpent Mound.

"Their plan to avoid disaster by building an effigy succeeded. As the mound took shape, the Great Snake in the sky began to fade. As the weeks passed, its tail grew shorter, its head grew dimmer. Finally, it disappeared.

"They had done it. Their Serpent Mound had turned the path of the Great Snake. Because of what they had achieved the earth had been spared.

"These people were not fools. They are to be envied. Think what it would mean to be deeply convinced that their actions had saved the world. They must have felt as the Athenians did after they defeated the Persians, twice. Or as America felt after World War Two.

"So there lay the Serpent Mound for a thousand years, its teal-blue eye staring upwards at the sky, day and night ... until the eye was stolen!

"When the earliest pioneers stumbled into southern Ohio and came upon the Serpent Mound, they had no idea what to make of it. Someone even theorized that it was placed there by God to indicate the Garden of Eden. They were immediately attracted by the Serpent's stony blue eye. They must have known the stone

18

didn't have the value of gold or silver or diamonds. Still, it might be worth something in a metropolitan area where jewelers would pay for semi-precious stones.

"Manhattan was the nearest such place in those days, but Manhattan was a long, long way off. Hauling the stone up the Ohio River to Pittsburgh would be arduous, and that was only the first leg of the journey. After that, it would have to be carried by wagon across the width of Pennsylvania and beyond. It certainly could not be sold for a profit sufficient to offset the cost of transporting it to New York City.

"Then, in 1825, the Erie Canal opened. It had been years in the making and it was the premier engineering marvel of the age.

"If the eye of the Serpent could be carried to Lake Erie, only 236 miles north from the Serpent Mound plateau, it could be shipped along the coast to Buffalo, from which it could be barged east on the new Canal to Albany, and then down the Hudson River to Manhattan, where jewelers knew a thing or two about semi-precious stones and would pay handsomely.

"Now, do you know about the River Pirates? Posing as honest traders, they would lure into their emporiums the settlers traveling by raft and flatboat down the Ohio River. They would kill these hapless victims, dump their bodies in the river and steal their belongings.

"Three such River Pirates – two brothers named Ethan and Simon Hackleshinn and another man named Ephraim Cutnaw – resolved to steal the eye of the Serpent and oomph it along in a sling as they made their way through the Ohio woods to Cleveland.

"Draw a line on a map of Ohio from Peebles, the village nearest the Serpent Mound today, on to the southernmost section of the shore of Lake Erie and you'll find that it cuts right across southern Richland County where you found your Blue Rock.

"Richland County was as far north as the three rascals had gotten when, exhausted and starving, they could not continue on until they re-supplied. They stopped in the middle of a dark forest. The evil brothers sent the equally nasty Ephraim to nearby Mansfield, a tiny village at that time, to purchase supplies.

"As soon as Ephraim was out of sight, the brothers conspired. They would kill Ephraim when he returned and split the profit from the sale of the Serpent's eye two ways instead of three.

"Ephraim, as he walked to Mansfield, had a similar thought. Why share the profit with the brothers when he could easily have it all to himself?

"In Mansfield, Ephraim bought hardtack, beans, and rice. Since all would be thirsty, he bought a jug of hard cider. But he also bought a vial of a deadly poison that the pioneers used to kill off skunks. Reaching the edge of town, he furtively emptied the poison into the jug of cider. Laughing, he shook the jug, good and hard.

"You can see what's coming. Ethan greeted Ephraim while Simon stole upon him from behind and fatally coldcocked him. The brothers, laughing, ate the hardtack while the beans and rice were cooking on the campfire. To wash down the hardtack, they swigged heavily from the jug. Within a half hour they both died in agony. The wolves and vultures made short work of the three carcasses.

"The Blue Rock must have been observed over the years by hunters who found it on the forest floor where the Hackle-shinns and Cutnaw had set it down, but neither they nor later settlers had the slightest notion that the Blue Rock had served for a thousand years as the eye of the Serpent Mound. Busy with planting, tending, and harvesting, they had little interest in the Blue Rock, and neither the inclination nor the means to inquire about its provenance. Transporting it to a New York jeweler does not seem to have occurred to them, or perhaps they were just more practical than their predecessors.

"The Blue Rock was still lying at the River Pirates' campsite when you came upon it fifty years ago, a century and a half later."

3

Holdfast Hale

IN A STATE OF WONDER, his mouth gaping, Walt Landgraf blinked several times and said, "You have found the *Blár Merki Steinn*. I'm certain of it."

"The what?"

"The *Blár Merki Steinn*. It's Old Norse. It means "Blue Boundary Stone." It was set down out there in Ohio by Holdfast Hale in 1663 to mark the southern boundary of the Western Reserve of Connecticut."

"Put there by a white man in 1663? That's awfully early for a white man to be in north-central Ohio."

"Yes and no. There were French Jesuit missions on the southern shore of Lake Erie by then. But it's true that white folks rarely ventured into the interior. And yet that is not the most amazing part of the story, not by a long shot. The whole tale is incredible from start to finish.

"I've known that story for years. Anybody who knows Connecticut history knows it. But I never knew the ending of the story.   And now you come along with your account of how you found what you call the Blue Rock. You seem to have added a new chapter to the tale."

"Would you tell it to me someday?" I asked enthusiastically.

"With pleasure," said Walt, "We're in no hurry. I'll tell it to you right now."

Walt leaned back in his rocking chair and crossed his legs.

We were seated together on the front porch of the White Hart Inn in Salisbury, Connecticut, where we had just enjoyed a fine dinner. Walt was a man of parts, an inspiring biology teacher at Litchfield High School for more than thirty years, a Scoutmaster, historian, and the dynamo behind the Barkhamsted Historical Society. Under his leadership, the Society restored the Squire's Inn and the Beckley Furnace and re-opened the Stone Museum in the People's State Forest. It was the site of many of Walt's lectures and programs as well as the trailhead for hikes he organized to teach others about nature and local history. He is fondly remembered and honored with a trail and a historic soapstone quarry named after him, both in Connecticut state parks.

Walt helped me bring to light *The Cabin Down the Glen*, a previously unpublished manuscript by Connecticut author Odell Shepard. I discovered this treasure among Shepard's papers at Trinity College's Watkinson Library. After I edited and published it, Walt helped me organize a "book launching" in Riverton, near the site of Shepard's "cabin down the glen."

Walt was in his early sixties when I knew him, bald and bespectacled. A smile constantly played about his lips. Even when he spoke seriously, you felt that a ripple of light laughter was imminent. He had insisted on taking Jo and me to the White Hart for dinner. His wife, a violinist, was away, he explained, at a chamber music festival in Nova Scotia.

"Edward the Confessor was the King of England for nearly a quarter century," Walt began, "but when he died in January of 1066, he left no heir to the throne.

"The council of royal advisors known as the *Witenagemot* appointed Harold Godwinson to the throne, but there were multiple other contenders, including his own brother Tostig Godwinson, and the King of Norway, Harald Hardrada.

"If all this seems far removed from your Blue Rock, bear with me. The story takes a while to unfold."

"Time," I said, quoting Thoreau, "is but the stream I go a-fishing in."

Walt laughed. "Good!" he said.

"When King Harald Hardrada of Norway got wind of Harold Godwinson's ascent to the throne, he was ticked off. The Norwegian king was buddies with Tostig Godwinson, and he thought that if he helped put Tostig on the throne of England, or – even better – if Tostig helped Hardrada to become king, then he could claim a good chunk of England for Norway as his reward. He ran the idea past Tostig, and Tostig was only too happy to join forces with him.

"So Tostig raised an army of Anglo-Saxons, and Harald Hardrada sailed to England from Norway with a fleet of three hundred ships. According to the account written afterwards by Leif the Longwinded, who came along on the trip, Harald brought with him one of the fabled *Blár Merki Steinner*. These were the 'Blue Boundary Stones' that marked the territory of Norway. The Vikings quarried these stones at the edge of a fjord in the northernmost regions of Norway and left them to mark the farthest points of their many invasions. Two or three have turned up in Newfoundland and Labrador. A half dozen or so have been found in France.

"Harald Hardrada intended to seize a sizeable fiefdom on the northeast coast of England and mark his ownership of it with a *Blár Merki Steinn*.

"The Norwegians landed in force near York, about nine thousand of them, where they met up with Tostig's army. The city fathers of York promptly surrendered to the combined invasion forces. To everyone's credit, there was no looting and the city fathers made sure all the soldiers were welcomed and well fed.

"Everything was going great for Tostig and Harald. There remained the question of which would become king, but they agreed to figure that out later.

"When King Harold Godwinson, back in London, learned that the Vikings had landed and that his brother Tostig had betrayed him, he headed north, headlong, with his housecarls and as many thanes as he could muster. They marched by day and night, making the 185-mile journey from London to Yorkshire in only four days. The speed of his march enabled Harold to take the Norwegians completely by surprise in their camp along the River Derwent.

"Too confident from their good fortune so far, Tostig and Harald had not even posted sentries, and until the English army came into view, they were completely ignorant of the proximity of a hostile army.

"To mount a full-scale attack, Harold had to get his army across the wooden Stamford Bridge that spanned the Derwent. Leif the Longwinded relates that a giant Norse axman blocked the narrow crossing and single-handedly held up the entire English army. If the story is to be believed, this solitary warrior cut down forty Englishmen. He was finally overcome only when an English soldier floated under the bridge in a half-barrel and thrust his spear through the bridge's planks into the giant's foot, immobilizing the heroic axman while the English mortally wounded him with multiple spear stabs.

"Then the English army stormed across the bridge. The fighting was fierce. Though the Norwegians had not had time to fully armor themselves, they formed one of their famous 'shield walls' and it held for a good while until ultimately it gave way. By nightfall the Norwegians and Tostig's army had been routed. Both Hardrada and Tostig, along with most of their men, were slain.

"The story of the battle is recounted from the English perspective in the anonymous *Anglo-Saxon Chronicle*. The Norwegian perspective gets its due in Leif the Longwinded's account and in the *Heimskringla*, the best known of the Old Norse sagas, written by Snorri Slumbersnot, the Icelandic poet, historian, and insomniac. (Variants of Snorri's surname appear in various spellings on the title pages of his other works, including Slumbershnott, Slumberzhnaught and Schlummernnicht.) All accounts aver that after the battle, Hardrada's *Blár Merki Steinn* came into the possession of Harold Godwinson.

"Leif, a Norwegian, had to be careful not to offend his patrons, so his account glosses over the loss of the *Blár Merki Steinn*. Snorri, being Icelandic, was not so constrained and gives more details. He tells how the arrogant Norsemen had brought the stone ashore, planning to position it deep in English territory to establish their claim. They left it on the beach when they marched on York, thinking they would come back for it to mark the eventual extent of their invasion.

"The Vikings who survived the battle of Stamford Bridge, scampering back to the beach as fast as they could, fled right past the *Blár Merki Steinn* and into the waves. They were frantic and exhausted, and the English were in hot pursuit. The Vikings clambered aboard the ships that were anchored nearest to the shore, with no thought of retrieving the *Blár Merki Steinn*.

"Some of the would-be invaders set the sails as fast as they could while others pulled on the oars with all their might, and when the English reached the beach, the Vikings were pulling away. Even so, English bowmen showered arrows upon the ships that were still in range, killing and wounding yet more Vikings. According to Snorri, the Vikings, who had arrived in three hundred ships, returned to Norway with only twenty-four. Naturally, Leif doesn't mention this.

"Snorri also relates that Harold Godwinson, coming upon the *Blár Merki Steinn* and realizing its intended use, stood on top of it in triumph, his sword held high, towering over his troops while the army cheered his victory.

"Though no one knew it that day, Harald Hadrada's attempted invasion was to be the last of the Viking raids of the Northern Seas. Their king was dead, their confidence was shattered, and their culture went into its fatal decline.

"Having soundly defeated his brother Tostig and Harald Hardrada at the Battle of Stamford Bridge, King Harold Godwinson seemed destined to be remembered as one of England's greatest hero-kings. By taking bold, quick action he had, in a single stroke, bested the Vikings once and for all and put down the rebellion his treacherous brother had sparked.

"He directed his men to gather the enemy's abandoned weapons and to bring them, along with the *Blár Merki Steinn*, back to London as evidence of his victory. We know this from the *Anglo-Saxon Chronicle*, which still exists, by the way.

"But Harold Godwinson's moment of glory was brief. The very day after the battle, while Harold's army was still resting, a messenger galloped into the English camp bearing dire news. William the Bastard, to be known ever afterward as 'The Conqueror,' had crossed the Channel and landed a sizeable army on England's south shore.

"Harold, ever the man of action, immediately force-marched his exhausted troops south. Worn out with marching, fighting, and then marching again, the English met William at the Battle of Hastings and, as the world knows, were defeated after a Norman arrow pierced Harold's eye and penetrated his brain. You can see Harold in the Bayeux Tapestry, falling off his horse with an arrow in his eye. William then marched his army to London where he was crowned king, beginning three hundred years of Norman rule over England.

28

"William, wanting to discredit Harold's victory at Stamford Bridge, did not put the *Blár Merki Steinn* on public display. Instead, he had it removed to the basement of the Tower of London where it remained, almost forgotten, for six centuries.

"Time marched on. Kings ascended to the English throne and departed in honorable and tragic ways. The Battle of Stamford Bridge, forever to be overshadowed by the Battle of Hastings, became a mere footnote in the history of Great Britain."

Jo and I hung on every word of Walt's account, but I was as eager as a kid to find out how the heck the *Blár Merki Steinn* was going to wind up in the woods of southern Richland County.

"We're still a long way from Ohio," I made bold to say.

Walt raised one finger. "Patience is the silent virtue," he said. "I warned you, it's a tale that takes some time in the telling.

"Come 1637, the English colony of Connecticut was established in the New World – in addition to a small, separate colony that called itself New Haven, yet another footnote in history. Because Connecticut was one of the less powerful and wealthy colonies, she had reason to worry that the wealthier and more powerful Massachusetts and New York would gobble up the lands that lay to their west.

"Connecticut had no wish to nibble into the territories of Massachusetts to the north nor New York to the south. She desired merely to retain, for future settlement, the lands to the west which she had long regarded as rightfully hers.

"Moreover, she feared that with Cromwell dead and Charles II restored to the throne, the new English government would attempt to assume absolute control over the Puritan colonies in New England. Her leaders decided, therefore, that their best hope for preserving their liberties, and the integrity of her westward territory, lay in petitioning the king for a legal charter that would affirm her status.

"Accordingly, John Winthrop Jr., Connecticut's duly elected governor, was chosen to lead the effort to accomplish this critically important task. John Winthrop Jr. was a man of wide-ranging interests – literary, political, philosophic, scientific, and mercantile – and even more important, a man of consummate tact, a born diplomat.

"Winthrop and a small committee made the dangerous crossing of the Atlantic in July of 1661, gained an audience with Charles II, and somehow persuaded the monarch to sign, on the twenty-third of April, the amazing Charter of Connecticut.

"The Charter gave Connecticut a freedom from the mother country such as no other British colony enjoyed either then or thereafter. It served as the basis for Connecticut's government for a hundred and fifty years.

"The Charter also guaranteed the Colony the possession of a narrow strip of land, one degree of latitude in width, stretching from Narragansett Bay all the way to the Pacific Ocean. Of course no one, least of all the vapid Charles II, knew how far the Pacific lay to the west of the Colony of Connecticut. But for the next century and a half, at least on paper, Connecticut was by far the largest of the seceding English colonies – fourteen of them, giving half-credit each to New Haven and Nova Scotia –

measuring seventy-five miles north to south and three thousand miles east to west. Let Texas and Alaska ponder that!

"Several other American colonies imagined their boundaries extending west to the Pacific. All of these were geographically and politically audacious, but Connecticut was the only one whose far 'western reserve' had a royal charter.

"The immediate benefits of the Charter to people of Connecticut were a clear legal basis for their colony; absorption of the New Haven Colony; and, most importantly, an exceedingly generous degree of self-government to the colonists. All the king asked in return was to receive one-fifth of any gold and silver that was mined in the colony.

"(That was not much of a compensation. As you may know, precious little gold or silver has ever been found, let alone mined, in Connecticut.)

"A glance at the map of the United States will show that, if today's southern boundary of Connecticut was to be extended westward it would slice right through the middle of north-central Ohio.

"Governor Winthrop felt that the southern boundary of Connecticut must be demarcated in a way that put the matter beyond dispute, immediately and for all time. He urged the placement of a boundary marker on that latitude, far to the west.

"King Charles seems to have agreed. As it happened, shortly after his ascent to the throne, the new King inspected the treasures housed in the Tower of London and was intrigued by the *Blár Merki Steinn* in the basement.

"Casting about for a suitable emblem to mark the colony's southern border, Charles II remembered the *Blár Merki Steinn*. He presented the stone to Governor Winthrop and his committee along with instructions to take it on their return voyage to Connecticut and to cause it to be placed at the exact latitude of the colony's southern border, five hundred miles to the west of the port of New Haven.

"(That municipality, though small, was nevertheless the largest settlement in the colony's southeastern-most corner, and the King felt that this recognition would answer whatever grumbling might result from its absorption into Connecticut.)

"The upshot was that the *Blár Merki Steinn* was to be placed in what is, today, north-central Ohio.

"Some Englishmen objected to Charles' idea of using the *Blár Merki Steinn* for this purpose. They considered it to be a prized emblem of British history, evidence of both the last victory of the Anglo-Saxons and the ending of the era of the Vikings. Many felt that the *Blár Merki Steinn* ought to remain in England in the possession of the English people.

"But Charles, like most people, loved his own ideas, if only for the simple reason that they were his. He did not need to defend his idea; but he did answer that the people of Connecticut were English too, and it was a far better use for the boundary stone than to gather dust in the Tower of London. The matter was easily settled. Charles, after all, was the king. But in fairness, since the original purpose of the *Blár Merki Steinn* was as a boundary marker, there was some justification to the King's idea.

"Governor Winthrop and his committee brought the stone when they returned to Connecticut in the autumn of 1662. When Winthrop announced the good news that he and the committee had succeeded in securing a charter for the Colony of Connecticut, he conveyed the King's command that the *Blár Merki Steinn* be placed five hundred miles west of New Haven, to remain for all time to designate the southern border of Connecticut's western reserve.

"Winthrop explained that the King's orders included a tribute of one-fifth of the gold and silver to be mined. As it seemed doubtful that any gold or silver would ever be mined in Connecticut, the governor deemed it all the more important that the *Blár Merki Steinn* be placed in keeping with the king's wishes.

"Winthrop asked for a volunteer to undertake the mission. The young hero who answered the call was Holdfast Hale, the scion of a prosperous and prominent New Haven family, famed in New England as makers of brick.

"Holdfast was a bluff and burly fellow, a familiar figure on the streets of New Haven. In his teenage years, his job in the family business was transportation of the product. As soon as newly made bricks were cool enough to handle, he would load a hundred of them onto his wooden wheelbarrow and push the vehicle along the cobble-stoned streets to a construction site, unload the bricks, and go back for more.

Doing this all day long, six days a week (resting on the Sabbath like the good Puritan he was), Holdfast attained the physique of a modern-day bodybuilder. It is said that his forearms and calves were equal in size to the hams of a fully grown hog and that his chest was of the size and hardness of an oak barrel.

"Probably the strongest man in the colony, Holdfast Hale was nevertheless a modest man and possessed a gentle disposition. New Haven knew that he was kind and friendly, and after he volunteered for the boundary stone mission he also became known as brave, even fearless.

"Not that he would ever admit it. In his later years, when people expressed their admiration for his courage, Holdfast would brush it off, saying that courage had nothing to do with what he had achieved and that his strength and perseverance were the gifts of a generous God.

"When Governor Winthrop announced the Connecticut Charter, it was mid-October and the leaves, just as beautiful then as they are in October today, were blazing out their reds and golds and purples. But this glory of nature also signaled that winter was at hand, so the governor insisted that Hale wait until spring before making the journey.

"And so it came to pass that on the first day of May 1663, Holdfast Hale hoisted the *Blár Merki Steinn* onto his wooden wheelbarrow, kissed his mother, embraced his father, patted his siblings on the head and cheered by his friends and neighbors and by Governor Winthrop himself, who had made the journey from Hartford to New Haven to see him off, Holdfast Hale headed west. He wore stout shoes and a Puritan's hat with a broad brim and a high crown. He carried a knife and a hatchet in his belt, a jug of water slung across his shoulder and a backpack containing a blanket and a good supply of hardtack, beans and rice.

"Paying with coins the governor had given him, Holdfast and his load were ferried across the Hudson River after which he disappeared into the Adirondacks. Leaving those mountains behind him at length, he entered regions where the farms were fewer and the woods were darker. The gravel roads gave way to dirt roads, which gave way to paths, which gave way to Indian trails.

"I wish I could give you a detailed account of Hale's epic journey to north-central Ohio and back. But he kept no diary and, later, when people asked about the adventures he had had, the obstacles he had overcome, the challenges of the weather and the terrain, he would only smile and say, 'It was all in God's hands.'

"He had to have encountered natives. Most likely, sensing his good nature, they fed him after his hardtack, beans and rice were gone. Their birchbark canoes could not have carried the *Blár Merki Steinn*, so Holdfast must have constructed rafts for crossing rivers. A great deal of hard pushing would have been required to oomph his heavily laden wheelbarrow over the Laurel Highlands of western Pennsylvania. One thinks of bears, wolves, and mountain lions. One thinks of rain and mud. One thinks of loneliness and homesickness.

"But as I said, we have no details of Hale's journey, save that his mission was accomplished. We know only that on September 16, 1663, he walked up to the front door of his family's home in New Haven, pushing his empty wooden wheelbarrow before him. And, as the people of New Haven love to tell, the very next day he was back on the cobbled streets of the growing town, pushing loads of new-made bricks to customers' jobsites.

"Holdfast Hale married and fathered a brood of burly offspring to whom he passed along his faith in God and his patriotism. You may have already guessed that his great-great-grandson was none other than Connecticut's greatest patriot, our officially designated state hero, the great and courageous Nathan Hale, a humble schoolteacher who acted as a spy during the American Revolution, and who, just prior to being executed by the British in September of 1776, uttered those deathless words learned by every American schoolchild, 'I only regret that I have but one life to lose for my country.'

"Now how about dessert and coffee? The White Hart is famous for its vanilla cheesecake with poached cherries!"

"Yum!" we said, and followed Walt back inside.

4

General Braddock

I TAUGHT FRENCH to high schoolers for six years. If you want to teach or learn a language, you have to have something to talk about. So using basic French I told my students about "*La Roche Bleue.*" They were fascinated and eager to see it when we hosted the French Club at our home for a picnic.

When you're teaching a language, what you talk about almost doesn't matter. We talked about things that interested me, and the students enlivened their intellects and warmed their imaginations as they drew near the flame of my passions.

In short sentences, using a limited French vocabulary, I related stories, jokes, anecdotes, and scenes from history. Questions were asked and answered in French. I brought props to the classroom, such as hats and costumes. We improvised skits in French. I taught them the basics of legerdemain. It was a blast for the kids, and not least, for me.

We also created dioramas together, babbling in French while we were at it. My favorite was the diorama we created to display the moment just prior to what came to be known as "Braddock's Defeat," one of the most dramatic battles of the French & Indian War.

One year, in the process of setting up the Braddock diorama, one of my best and brightest students, Maddie Pourvakil, offered a theory about the provenance of the Blue Rock. Her explication of it astonished me.

We arranged the diorama on three large tables, placed end to end, spanning the classroom. We used toy soldiers and accessories from my large collection of such things. (From my boyhood days, I have loved military miniatures. Believing, rightly, that playing with toy soldiers would spark interest in history, my parents gave me sets of the Marx toy soldiers with which some kids played back then. I still have them all. Several thousand *petites soldats*.)

For my high-schoolers, these were exotic objects. Not a single student had played with toys like these. I told them how I would set up hundreds of my toy soldiers on my bedroom floor and fight long battles that went on for days.

I have toy horses for the soldiers to ride, cannons and caissons, and little houses and forts for them to besiege, surrender, and recapture. I have little green plastic trees and little gray plastic boulders for them to hide behind, waiting to ambush their opponents. Fences, too. I can build castles out of wooden blocks, made by my father for me sixty-five years ago. I brought my blocks to class, and we built chateaux.

My toy soldiers represent many eras and places. I have blue and gray Civil War soldiers. I have dark blue U.S. Cavalry soldiers who sit on little black rubber saddles, mounting brown horses. They fought against the Indians, reddish tan. I have silver-gray knights-in-armor and green figures of Robin Hood,

Little John, fat Friar Tuck and the Merry Men. I have figures of Good King Richard, his evil brother King John, and the Sheriff of Nottingham.

I have a set of blue soldiers of the French Foreign Legion, a desert fort, palm trees for an oasis, and gray and brown Arabs who ride horses and camels. I have pirates of many different colors, and I built ships out of blocks for them to board, plunder and burn.

I have a miniature Alamo that came with blue Mexican soldiers and tan American frontiersmen in brown buckskin. I have a set of Zorro figures. I also have soldiers of World War Two, the war my father fought in. The American soldiers are dark green, and their enemies, the Nazis, are gray. I could fight the battles of the American Revolution, too, with the light blue soldiers of the Continental Army and their enemy, the "lobster-backs," the British Redcoats.

My collection includes historic personages, too. I have a little General Grant and a little General Lee. They confer over a little plastic table when Lee surrenders to Grant at Appomattox, their staffs lined up and watching on either side. I have a little Abraham Lincoln who meets his generals in front of a gray plastic tent, as in the famous photograph of Lincoln and McClellan after Antietam.

I have figures of George Washington and General Cornwallis, who surrendered at Yorktown. I have Davy Crockett, Daniel Boone, and the Lone Ranger. I have a dashing little figure of George Armstrong Custer, wearing a fringed leather coat, his cowboy hat turned up on one side, his long yellow hair tumbling down in back. He has blue trousers with a bright yellow stripe down the sides, and he wears shiny black cavalry boots. Desperate, he is firing a pistol.

To create the diorama of Braddock's Defeat we placed my plastic model of Fort Apache at the far end of the tables. We transformed it into Fort Duquesne with a penciled sign taped above the gate. Next to it, we made an Indian camp with teepees and a campfire and Indians in canoes. With blue construction paper, we modeled the "Forks of the Ohio," the mighty meeting of the Ohio, Allegheny, and Monongahela, the three great rivers which join majestically at present-day Pittsburgh.

French regulars in blue and white uniforms, the colors of the Bourbon Kings, manned the fort along with Canadian militia. The approaching British and colonial column covered two tables. General Braddock himself was in the lead, mounted on a horse, waving his sword. His redcoats marched close behind him, including drummers and bagpipers in kilts. Cannons were mounted on caissons pulled along by horses. Behind those came the Virginia militia, and it was easy to spot young George Washington at the head of its column. Behind the Virginians, we placed six covered wagons with horses and drivers, transporting the army's supplies. One of the teamsters was nineteen-year-old Daniel Boone, so we placed on that wagon seat my Daniel Boone figure, in his trademark fringed jacket and coonskin cap.

On both sides of this long procession, we placed plastic trees and rocks to represent the dense, dark forests of Pennsylvania through which the British hacked and chopped, building a corduroy road as they went along, advancing only two miles a day.

Behind the trees and rocks the Indians hid and waited alongside French regulars and French-Canadian militia. We created the moment just before the attack; there were no dead or wounded soldiers in our diorama. All were alive and fit and about to fulfill their destiny.

We described and discussed all this in French, looking up words that were new to us when we needed them. It was a great way to expand our vocabulary and to practice our grammar. One might think high-schoolers would fancy themselves "too cool" for such things, but they all loved creating the diorama of Braddock's Defeat and were completely absorbed by what we were doing.

(Ah, I loved teaching. Then the COVID-19 pandemic came along and sidelined my teaching career. None of the activities we relished in the classroom could be replicated in Zoom sessions. Now I teach elders in the University of Cincinnati's lifelong learning program. We do the same fun stuff, including the diorama of Braddock's Defeat, but they can't muster the hilarity and energy of my teenaged students.)

I digress.

To fully appreciate Maddie Pourvakil's ingenious theory of the Blue Rock's origin and destiny, the details of Braddock's Defeat must first be understood. Let me tell you what I told my students.

"Great Britain was at war with France as the two empires competed in the colonizing of the world. The French were smarter in some ways. The French, greatly outnumbered by the British colonists, made friends with the American Indians, whom they needed as allies and trading partners. In turn, the Indians taught the French guerrilla warfare.

"General Edward Braddock, commanding the British and Colonials, was a brave and competent soldier. His command, made up of smartly uniformed British regulars and rag-tag Colonial volunteers, was motivated and ready for action. But the action Braddock had seen on the battlefields of Europe had not prepared him to fight the French and Indians in the American wilderness, and worse yet, he would not be bothered with advice on the subject.

"He sat tall on his saddle like the English gentleman he was, resplendent in a handsome red coat with two rows of shiny brass buttons and pristine white cross belts over his chest. He wore a striking crimson sash around his middle and a black hat with bright white trim. A shining sword hung from his belt. If ever there were a perfect target for guerrillas, it was General Braddock.

"Braddock and his men, under orders to seize Fort Duquesne, did not try to sneak up on the French and their Indian allies. Not at all! They marched into the woods with drums beating and bagpipes playing. They were loud and proud because they supposed they were invincible.

"Young Colonel George Washington, who knew a thing or two about wilderness combat, had tried to warn Braddock, but the General would not listen. Few expected anything less than a complete victory. Not even wise old Benjamin Franklin, who had overseen the supplying of the army back in Philadelphia, foresaw the disaster that was at hand.

"The forest itself was an enemy, densely overgrown and filled with shadows. The army could move only as fast as the log road could be built. It was summertime, and the axmen took off their crimson red coats and rolled up the sleeves of their bright white shirts.

"While the British and colonial army made its noisy way, axes chopping and trees falling and drums beating and bagpipes playing, the French and the Indians hid noiselessly and watched their red-coated enemies.

"The Indians were very skilled at hiding. They peeked at the British from behind ferns and through crevices of rocks and branches of trees. They waited for the perfect time and place to attack.

"On the last day he was ever to lead an army, General Braddock was riding just behind the axmen. They were about ten miles from Fort Duquesne. He was hoping his army would come to an open meadow in front of the fort where he could line up his cannons and infantry like chess pieces and defeat the French in a 'civilized' battle as he had done so successfully in Europe.

"The British and Colonials numbered about 2200, and the French knew that from Indian scouts. For their part, the French had only 300 regulars plus Indians and militia, perhaps 1600 in all. You might wonder why the French, so outnumbered, didn't just stay in the safety of their fort and wait to stave off an attack. They could not afford to. Their scouts had seen the large contingent of British artillery, which could easily demolish their stockade. The French had to attack.

"On came the British and the colonists, hacking their way through the wilderness. Suddenly shots came from nowhere, and several British axmen dropped to the ground. Just as suddenly came whoops and hollers as the Indians rushed forward from their hiding places, tomahawks and spears and knives flashing.

"The French continued to fire from their hiding places, reloading their muskets and firing again as fast as they could. The General's horse reared, pierced by French bullets. The General fell with his horse but got up and ran back toward the rest of his army.

"The British and colonials had heard the shots, the screams of the wounded, and the shrieks of the Indians, but they couldn't form ranks as they had been trained because the road was too narrow. They did not even return fire, having been trained not to shoot back unless ordered to do so.

"Their officers tried to form them into short lines, at least, and a few fired back at random; but soon, dense gun smoke hung in the forest like a fog, further hiding the French and Indians. During the entire battle, the British barely glimpsed their assailants.

"The British and Colonials turned and fled in terror. Many of them were killed as they ran, shot in the back by the French and Indian sharpshooters. Braddock himself was shot through the lungs, his ravaged body carried along by the retreating troops as they ran. The army was falling apart, and it looked like every British soldier would be killed.

"Then a tall, cool-headed and young colonial colonel only twenty-two years old, whose name you know, took charge. His manner was strong and steady. He commanded the soldiers to stop running, formed them up with some kneeling in front and others standing behind, and commenced to return fire. Some of the Indians, charging out from their hiding places, were shot and killed as were a few of the French.

"The army was retreating, yes, but they were no longer running away in panic. They kept up their return fire, and the French and Indians began to melt away. The British and colonials moved in an orderly fashion, making their way back to safety. The young colonel returned with about half the army and soon became known as the Hero of the Monongahela. He would later be remembered as the Father of his Country. Who was he?"

Up to this point, my students were spellbound, their eyes wide, their heads tilted in thought. Now, questioned, they bestirred themselves. "George Washington!" they instantly responded.

"Four days later, Braddock died of his wounds with Washington at his side. His dying words were 'Who would have thought?' The general admitted to the young Colonel Washington that he had been wrong not to listen to him, presenting Washington with his blood-stained sash.

"Washington forever kept the sash with him. He wore it when he accepted the surrender of the British at Yorktown, and again when he was inaugurated as the first American president. It is displayed today at Washington's home, Mount Vernon."

Quite a story, *n'est-ce pas*? Imagine it told in our classroom, in simple French, the students following it with rapt attention.

When I finished, Maddie Pourvakil spoke up. I could see by her face that she was entranced, and knowing her to be creative, precociously verbal, surprisingly knowledgeable, and a born storyteller, I let her proceed. Due to her excitement, she spoke mostly in English, and of course that was OK.

"Braddock had along with him a large blue rock," she assertively began.

"Yes!" cried the other students, turning toward her. They knew they were in for another of the great stories Maddie would sometimes improvise in class.

"The stone had been owned and cherished by the Braddock family for generations. According to family legend, one of the general's illustrious ancestors had discovered it when he stubbed his toe while visiting Stonehenge. It had been buried in the ground there for no one knows how long, probably many centuries.

"Braddock's ancestor, also a general, looked down to see what he had tripped on and saw, to his surprise, the tip of a bright blue rock. He had soldiers of his command dig it up, and it proved to be remarkably large and heavy. Despite its size, Braddock's ancestor carried the blue rock with him for luck in his campaigns, wherever he went. The blue rock became the family's talisman.

"General Braddock carried it with him too, everywhere he went. He believed that keeping it near to hand accounted, at least in part, for his long string of successes on the battlefields of Europe. On the long march to Fort Duquesne, he ordered it to be loaded into the very wagon driven by Daniel Boone, the most trustworthy and resourceful of his teamsters, along with a small fortune in gold coins which Braddock had brought to bribe the French and their Native American allies, if necessary.

"Colonel Washington, fearing an attack, had instructed young Boone to keep his precious cargo secure at all costs. So when Boone heard the shouting and gunfire a half-mile ahead, he quickly pulled his wagon off the road and drove about a hundred yards into the woods. A handful of Virginia militiamen came with him. They hid in the woods all that day, listening but, owing to the density of the forest, seeing nothing. They would not have dared shoot and reveal their position, but in any event, they saw no one to shoot.

"With night, silence fell, and Boone's company looked at one another, trying to think what to do. They could not return to the road: it would be patrolled by the French and Indians. They could make their way east, back toward the British colonies on the seacoast, but that is what their enemies would be expecting stragglers to do: the hostile Indian tribes in central Pennsylvania would surely be on the lookout for them. The only option for Boone and his men was to head west into the Ohio country."

"Here we go!" said another student. "The Blue Rock is headin' for Ohio."

"Their wagon was too wide and too heavy to be pulled through the forest. So that night Boone and his men stole back to the scene of the battle and returned with an abandoned British caisson, small and light enough to be pulled by a single horse. They oomphed Braddock's talismanic blue rock and their treasury of gold coins onto the caisson. The next morning, they marched west on foot, leading one horse pulling the caisson and two others carrying burlap bags full of hardtack, beans and rice recovered from an abandoned supply wagon.

"The journey was arduous, but they made it undetected to the Ohio River. There they again considered their options. They could build a raft and float along to the southwest, letting the current carry them downstream to the Mississippi and south to New Orleans. But there were no British outposts on the Ohio; and Louisiana, being a French colony, was hostile.

"So they decided to cross the Ohio River and make their way north to Lake Erie, where the Catawba tribe lived. The Catawbas were neutral in the war between Great Britain and France because they wanted to continue trading with both sides. As it happened, Boone spoke the Catawba language and convinced his companions that their party would be welcomed or at least tolerated.

"All the while, Boone suspected that his party was being trailed by Indian scouts, and their whereabouts reported back to the French, who still held Fort Duquesne. The French had to prepare for what they knew was coming: another British army would be sent, sooner or later, to take Fort Duquesne, and their leadership would be smarter this time. But the tiny remnant of the invading army, led by Boone and fleeing through the Ohio country, held little interest for the French and their Indian allies, and in fact they were not followed.

"Boone's company supplemented their diet of hardtack, beans and rice by shooting wild game. One day, the crack of one of Boone's rifle shots reached the ears of a Cherokee villager near present-day Bellville. The Cherokees, like the Catawba, were neutral in this war, but they knew well to distrust white men of any stripe who crossed their territory without permission. So a party of Cherokee warriors was dispatched to follow Boone's party to ensure that they did not stop permanently to found a settlement.

"The hot-headed young Cherokee warriors, eager to prove themselves by returning with prizes, managed to steal the Boone company's three horses while the unsuspecting frontiersmen made camp in what is today southern Richland County."

"The future home of Mr. Sowash!" said a student.

"Yep," I said. I was relishing Maddie's story just as much as the rest of her young listeners.

"Without their horses and the caisson," Maddie continued, "they could no longer transport their gold coins and the blue rock. So they did the only logical thing. They buried most of the gold coins in the fertile soil of Richland County and placed the blue rock to mark the spot. They dispatched the caisson down the steep slope of a ravine, and it broke to pieces on the rocks in the stream bed at the bottom.

"The Boone company continued on their way, unharmed, finally arriving at the southern shore of Lake Erie, where they were cautiously greeted by the Catawbas. Eventually, the party made their way back to the British colonies on the seacoast.

"Boone always meant to return to the Ohio wilderness to retrieve the treasure, but he was too busy discovering the Cumberland Gap and leading settlers into Kentucky."

"Becoming an American icon in the process," I interjected.

"He never made it back to Richland County. On his deathbed, Boone tried to describe the location to his sons but there was no map. He said he would know the place if he saw it, but he couldn't be specific enough about the lay of the land or any landmarks. So, possessing only the most vague of directions, his sons never even tried to find it.

"All of this brings me to an important question for you, Mr. Sowash. When you discovered '*La Roche Bleue*,' did it occur to you to dig beneath it, to see if it marked the site of a buried treasure?"

I looked at Maddie and shook my head abjectly. "No," I said. "Fool that I was, it never occurred to me."

"Do you think you could still find the exact spot where you found it?"

"Doubtful," I said with a sigh. "It's been many years and I am sure I could no longer locate the place where it lay. Honestly, I'm not completely sure which woods it was. The only thing I can recall with any certainty is that it was in the large wooded area that lies between the village of Butler on the east side, the village of Bellville on the west side, the Clear Fork River on the north side and the tiny hamlets of Ankenytown and Palmyra to the south."

Maggie, saddened as well, recovered her composure. "So Boone's treasure will just have to remain there until ... until ... until the next Ice Age comes along and the glaciers come down from the north once more and push the gold coins south to the places where they will lay, scattered in the soil, until someone from some future civilization comes upon them."

"Well done and well told, Maddie," I said, impressed.

I began clapping and all her classmates ardently joined in.

5

Lorenzo da Ponte

BIFF TRILLER is one of my closest friends. He is a talented guy. An extraordinary choral director, trumpeter, and baritone soloist, he is equally at home with the guitar or a piano. He abounds with energy and organizes an annual concert by the October Festival Chorus, which he founded. He is the Minister of Music at our church, Mt. Auburn Presbyterian, where he directs the chancel choir and provides splendid music for services year-round. He has a boyish, fun-loving manner and is loved by everyone who knows him.

An ardent champion of my music, Biff has performed or directed the premiere performances of about thirty of my works, some of which are dedicated to him. He premiered my twelve-movement cantata for soloists, chorus, and instrumental ensemble, *The Harvest of a Quiet Eye*, one of my best works, and he organized and directed another performance of it ten years later. He has recorded my music, too, on several occasions.

Biff loves books and poetry and ends every choir rehearsal by reading a poem and then offering a prayer. He loves, as I do, the history of music. If there is a more fascinating subject, I have not found it. The story of how we humans have rendered intricate metaphors from pure abstract sound will pin your ears back. Too, the story of music is replete with fantastical and outrageous personalities.

He doesn't look like a choir director or any other kind of musician. The crown of his head and most of his face always appear to have been left unshaven for three days. From his solid build and manly bearing you'd guess he was a retired stevedore, large-animal veterinarian, or brewery delivery man. He wears glasses but, as he says, "only when I want to see."

Biff owns a pickup truck and he's glad to come round with it to help when something must be transported that's too big to fit in the trunk of a car. When we bought our home, some furnishings came along with it, including a king size bed. When we added French doors to the rear of the house, the bed was too large for the newly configured room; it blocked the access to the French doors. So we sold it online to a woman who asked that we deliver it to her house a few miles away. I phoned Biff and, like the good friend he is, he came round with his truck.

The bed delivered, we returned to my house and ensconced ourselves in the pavilion in our upper garden, each equipped with a cold beer. We sipped and talked and laughed. Soon enough, as you can guess, the conversation came round to the Blue Rock.

"And you say this Blue Rock is here, on your property?" he asked.

"Yep. It's in the lower garden in plain sight from where you're sitting."

Biff looked about him. When someone is looking for it, it's easy to spot. He got up and went over to it. Down on one knee, he gave it a close inspection.

"This is not rock," he said. "It's slag."

"It's what?"

"Slag. It's a rock-hard waste material that separates out as part of any ore smelting and refining process. This particular stuff looks like it came from a glassmaking plant."

"But there are no glassmaking operations up in north-central Ohio. So how did it get there?"

He looked at it again, thoughtfully. It held his gaze for a long time. "I am pretty sure that I know exactly what this is and how it got there," he said in a low, almost conspiratorial voice. "You say you found it lying on the forest floor?"

"Yep. I see you were listening. You get an A!"

"What you have here, Maestro Sowash, is *Scoria Azzurra*. That's Italian for "azure slag." It's the congealed residue that's thrown away after Venetian artisans have finished rendering Murano glass, the most beautiful glassware ever made. Only this isn't just any "azure slag." You found and brought home a legendary treasure. In itself, even Murano slag has no value, but this has got to be *the* azure slag, *La Scoria Azzurra*. It was once the cherished possession of Lorenzo Da Ponte. Have you heard of him?"

"You don't mean Mozart's librettist?"

"Exactly. You know your music history! As it happens, I just finished reading Da Ponte's biography last week, and he was a truly remarkable man. I am convinced that your Blue Rock was his *Scoria Azzurra.*

"Lorenzo was born into a Jewish family in Venice in the mid-eighteenth century and given the name Emanuele Conegliano. His father Geronimo was a master glassmaker on the Venetian island of Murano. He was among the very few who knew the closely guarded secret process for making the exquisite Murano blue glassware.

"When Emanuele was in his early teens, his mother died, and his father converted himself and his three sons to Roman Catholicism so that he would be permitted to marry a Catholic woman with whom he'd fallen in love.

"In that time and place, as a part of the baptism ritual, a converted Jew was given the name of the bishop who baptized him, and so Emanuele Conegliano became Lorenzo Da Ponte.

"Bishop Da Ponte took a lively interest in his brilliant young protégé and got him enrolled in a seminary where he was ordained a priest, became a professor of literature, and taught Latin, Italian and French.

"Young Lorenzo did not strictly observe the vows he had taken. He took a mistress, with whom he had two daughters. In time, this became public knowledge, and he was brought to trial on a charge of 'public concubinage' and 'abduction of a respectable woman.' He was also charged with living in a brothel and organizing entertainments for the clientele, which seems to have been true. The judges found him guilty and banished him from Venice.

"At supper on the night before Lorenzo's departure, his aging father, in keeping with an ancient custom among the Murano glassmakers, presented his son with an extraordinary mass of iridescent azure-tinted slag from the glass works. 'I fell in love with the color and striation in this piece,' said old Geronimo. 'It looks just like the blueberry dessert you loved so much, the one that Mama used to make. It will serve as a reminder of your youth. Keep it with you until you can pass it on to your own eldest son or, having no son, to a youth you deem worthy.' The precious lump was to remain in Da Ponte's possession for the next thirty years.

"Da Ponte relocated to Austria, where he made a living of sorts as a writer, kissing up to aristocrats. He landed a gig translating opera librettos, which led to his meeting Mozart and Salieri. The latter used his influence to have Da Ponte appointed the official librettist of the Italian Theatre in Vienna. Mozart became a close friend, and Da Ponte always maintained that Mozart was the only man he ever met who could beat him at billiards.

"In the next few years, he wrote the librettos for Mozart's most popular Italian operas, *The Marriage of Figaro*, *Don Giovanni*, and *Cosi Fan Tutte*. To this day they are, as you know, among the greatest librettos and operas.

"The two friends had plans for more operas, but Mozart tragically died, only thirty-six years old. And not long after that, accused of shady dealings – history is unclear about the details of this charge – Da Ponte was removed from his post as the official Viennese Italian Theatre librettist.

"He made his way to Prague, then Dresden, then Paris – with a letter of recommendation to Queen Marie Antoinette, which he had finagled from her brother, the late Emperor. But the French Revolution was picking up steam, so he headed for the safety of London instead. At his side was his beautiful and buxom companion, Nancy Grahl, who bore him four daughters in rapid succession.

"In London Da Ponte tried his hand as a grocer, an Italian teacher, a publisher, and an impresario, finally becoming the librettist at the King's Theatre. Despite all his efforts, or perhaps because of them, he was forced into bankruptcy and, dodging debtor's prison, he fled next to New York City with Nancy and their daughters.

"In New York he opened a bookstore, a surefire way to lose money. One of his customers was Clement Clarke Moore, a leading intellectual of the day. Moore later wrote 'The Night Before Christmas,' the only thing he's remembered for today. The two became close friends, and Moore secured a post for Da Ponte as the first professor of modern languages at Columbia University. Not only was he the first Roman Catholic to join the Columbia faculty, but he was also the first of Jewish lineage. For the time, this was very progressive on the part of Columbia, probably the only university in America that would have hired such a person.

"By all accounts, Da Ponte was a remarkable teacher. He was fondly remembered by his students for bringing to the classroom colorful hats and costumes, a puppet theater, dioramas of famous battles. They also warmly remembered his providing morning classes with a generous spread of pastries and coffee.

"His students all recalled the game he invented to teach them Italian, which he called *Il Gioco della Descrizione,* or 'The Description Game.' He brought the *Scoria Azzurra* from his home to the classroom. Then he oomphed the much-prized slag onto a table in the center of the room and asked his students to form a circle around it. Under his direction, they took turns describing its attributes, saying in Italian, 'The Scoria is blue' or 'The Scoria is hard' or 'The Scoria is beau-tiful.' An adjective, once used, could not be repeated, and thus the students were forced to venture more and more deeply into the language as they sought out words to describe the object.

"When a student offered a description deemed too outlandish, he had to defend it, in Italian, and then the other students voted on whether to deem it acceptable. 'The Scoria is sad,' for example, was disqualified after a lively discussion. Disqualified players could still vote, and one by one the remaining students were removed. The last student standing, so to speak, was declared the winner and given a bottle of Chianti.

"Da Ponte's star student was Bentham Willoughby, whose later mastery of Native American languages led to the establishment of anthropology as a respected field of study. The aging librettist, having no son of his own, took a special interest in the young man and passed many hours with him outside the classroom, mentoring him, recounting the episodes of his life, and offering the benefit of his wisdom and counsel.

"Always restless, Da Ponte left teaching after a few years and poured his energy into the introduction of opera to New York City. He produced the first full performance of *Don Giovanni* on this side of the Atlantic.

"He founded the first opera theater in New York City and in America, which he named the Italian Opera House. However, not surprisingly, due to Da Ponte's lavish lifestyle and lack of common sense, the theater closed after only two seasons and was sold to pay off debts. It was, all the same, the immediate predecessor of and inspiration for the New York Metropolitan Opera.

"With his theater closed and his bookstore liquidated, probably to dodge creditors, the aging Da Ponte headed west to seek his fortune. He ventured as far west as Sunbury, Pennsylvania, where he opened an emporium selling provisions to pioneers heading west in ox-drawn Conestoga wagons.

"One day, Da Ponte, wearing an apron at the counter in the grocery, looked up from his cashbox to see a familiar face. It was Bentham Willoughby, a few years older but instantly recognizable. The friends embraced and passed several days together, laughing, playing billiards, and drinking wine. Willoughby had invested in a Conestoga wagon and was going west to study the languages of the natives. Da Ponte, though practically penniless, generously stocked Willoughby's wagon with hardtack, beans and rice from his shelves.

"On the last evening before Willoughby's departure, Da Ponte, realizing this dear young friend came as close to being a son as he would likely have, presented his promising former student with *La Scoria Azzurra*, remembering his father's charge. He wished the young man safety and success, and his expectation that the *Scoria* would bring him good luck. Tears in their eyes, the teacher and former student embraced for the last time and made their farewell.

"Two months later, Willoughby reached Ohio. But one stormy night, not far from the Cherokee village he meant to visit, he lost his way in the dark and strayed into a dense forest. Leaves were falling so thickly that the road was obscured. He ran off the road and the wagon overturned, spilling its contents onto the forest floor. With practically no light, he rigged his horses to one side of the wagon and was able to right it. But it was still mired in the mud, and it was only by discarding, with much regret, the heavy *Scoria Azzurra* that Willoughby was finally able to continue on his way. He left the precious object on the forest floor, intending to return for it someday. He never did.

"Da Ponte eventually returned to New York and became an American citizen, one of our most colorful and illustrious. When he died in 1838 at the age of eighty-nine, his funeral ceremony was the most enormous occasion of its kind the city had seen. It was held in St. Patrick's Cathedral, and Da Ponte, always a man of the theater at heart, would have surely appreciated that his passing drew a crowd described as 'standing room only.'"

6

Blue Jacket

"DOES THE NAME WEYAPIERSENWAH mean anything to you?"

"Say what?"

"Weyapiersenwah," Mark Hopper said again.

The process of purchasing the 1830 Greek Revival farmhouse that is now our home required a termite inspection. Mark Hopper was the inspector. He parked on the street, and I met him on the brick walk that leads to our pillared front porch.

"What a beautiful house!" was the first thing he said.

"Yes! Thank you! We think so, too."

He stopped at the brass plaques posted on the wall next to the front door and studied them with great interest.

The National Register of Historic Places plaque is standard.

The larger plaque is like a museum interpretive sign:

"Wow," he said. And he meant it.

I was by his side as he examined each room, the second floor "cubbyhole" that was to be "my room" and every inch of the foundation, both outside and in the basement. He found no evidence of termites.

Mark never ceased to marvel at what he saw. He loved it all and exclaimed, again and again, at the woodwork, the paneling in the dining room, the thick and heavy old doors, the pine floors, the exposed beams.

The supporting cross beams in the basement made him gasp. He pulled out a tape measure and exclaimed, "These beams are almost four inches thick and eighteen inches wide! And twenty feet long! Do you realize how big and old these trees were?" He shook his head. "I see a lot of houses in my line of work, and this one is just plain extraordinary!"

The termite inspection took place in October of 2019 when the previous owners were still living in the home. Their antiques were beautifully suited to the home, but they were not our antiques. "You'll have to come back sometime," I told him, "after we've moved in and have our own antiques in place and our collections on the shelves."

"I would *love* to come to this house again," said Mark, giving me his card and an estimate of his fees for an annual inspection.

I liked Mark right away. He was shorter than I and wiry in build, and he moved with a confident grace. He had twinkling eyes, sandy hair, and a successful mustache. (A mustache, to be termed successful, must be at least three times as thick as the eyebrows on the same face.) I kept his card.

But imagine my astonishment at church a few days later. I always arrive early and stay late because I love to socialize with my fellow congregants, a bright and caring bunch of folks. When Bill Bogdan spotted me, he came bustling up and said, "You know Mark Hopper?"

I had to think for a moment. "The termite inspector?"

"Yes! He came to our house right after he was at the property you're planning to buy, and he couldn't stop raving about the place. How historic and beautiful it was. And when he mentioned that the prospective new owner was a certain 'Rick Sowash,' we said, 'We know him!'"

What a coincidence! In a county of 800,000 people, Mark, having just met me, went across town and struck it up with one of my dearest church pals.

We were glad to learn that the house was free of termites, but even if Mark had discovered a major infestation of the vermin, we would have bought the property and dealt with the termites afterwards. We loved this house from the moment we entered it and knew, to our cores, that it would be ideal as our final home, the last domicile we'd share in our long marriage. We knew we would be very happy here – as, indeed, we have been – and so we bought the house.

One morning the following summer I looked out my window from the "cubbyhole." There is a beautiful view from there, down into our gardens and on through the tall old pines behind them to acres and acres of rolling greenswards beyond. A mile off, the western slope of the Little Miami River Valley rises, heavily wooded and usually a little hazy in the morning.

Then I noticed some odd little fuzzy bits of wood on the window sill. I brushed them off into my hand and tossed them in the wastebasket. The next morning, they were there again. What was going on? In a word, hornets.

I called in Mark Hopper to deal with the problem, and I held his ladder while he climbed onto the roof. The hornets had made their nest in the seam where one of our three brick chimneys meets the shingles. He dealt with it, instructing me to wait until evening and then to seal up the seams with caulk and roofing tar.

Mark was very eager to see the inside of the house again and I gave him the grand tour. He hovered over our furniture and collections, listening with close attention. He loved it all.

Friends have said our home is "a museum of American folk art, only way cozier than any museum could be." Another friend called it "Baby Monticello."

There is a cherry drop-leaf table in the wood-paneled dining room. Around it are six sturdy, mid-19th-century chairs decorated with hand-painted dogwood blossoms. A cherry corner-cupboard with wavy glass windows stands in the corner (where else)?

A log cabin quilt, made by my wife's great-great-great-grandmother when she was nine years old, hangs on the wall in the guest room. Paintings, prints and hand-hooked rugs adorn the plain plaster walls in every room. Woolen area rugs lie on polished pine floors. Redware, "Flow Blue" china, and Native American ceramics grace the shelves in some rooms, pewter mugs and carved shorebirds in others. The gems of my collection of hand-painted toy soldiers are on display in my "cubbyhole."

A fire-screen that I made long ago closes off the fireplace during the warmer months. It displays a "tree of life" rendered in little pieces of wood, painted and glued into place: a brown trunk and branches, green leaves, red apples, birds, a robin's nest, and a scampering gray squirrel.

We hope to celebrate the house's two-hundredth birthday in 2030. It's the perfect place for our collections, a folk-art museum indeed. When I was a boy, one of the many things I wanted to be some day was director of a museum. Now I live in one!

Mark loved our gardens no less than he loved our house and furnishings. It's such a pleasure to share all this with such an enthusiastic visitor. I walked with him around the formal, symmetrical upper garden with the Greek Revival pavilion placed in the center above a brick pavement. I showed him the lower garden too, a "transitional woodland garden" with a heavy mulch of pine needles that drop from the trees above. He admired the little Provençal fountain that sits at the stone boundary wall that separates the two gardens.

Then he spotted the Blue Rock.

"What's this?" he wanted to know.

"It takes a bit of explaining. Are you in a hurry? Let's sit in the rockers in the pavilion. I'll get us a couple cups of coffee and then I'll tell you all about it."

Coffee in hand, I told him the story of how I had come to possess the Blue Rock. Mark became more and more fascinated. When I finished, he was quiet for a long moment.

He broke his silence by asking, "Does the name Weyapiersenwah mean anything to you?"

As I have already said, it did not.

Then he asked another question. "What was the worst defeat ever inflicted upon the U.S. Army by Native Americans?"

"Was it Custer's Last Stand?"

"That's what everybody guesses. But no, it wasn't. Custer's folly brought down 268 US cavalrymen. More than three times that number were killed at the Battle of the Wabash. It wasn't really a battle; it was a rout. It was the worst defeat by Native Americans in the history of the American military, yet few Americans today have even heard of it. You might have heard it mentioned by the name Americans gave it afterwards, St. Clair's Defeat. Weyapiersenwah was the Shawnee war chief who, along with Miami Chief Little Turtle, led a coalition of Native tribes to victory."

I nodded and said I had indeed heard of St. Clair's Defeat and knew the outline of the story.

"You like history," Mark went on. "You've probably read the books of Allan Eckert, right?"

"I read *The Frontiersman*, about Simon Kenton, and I liked it a lot, but I never went on to read Eckert's other books."

"I liked that book, too," said Mark. "It was the first one I read. In fact, I liked it so much that I went on to read everything Eckert wrote. And I didn't stop there. You might say I'm obsessed with the history of the Old Northwest. I've been reading everything I can find about for years now. I think I know what your Blue Rock is, and why it was located where you found it. But first I have to refresh your memory of the details of St. Clair's Defeat.

"The Natives gave the American army a terrible whipping that day, and it all happened about a three-hour drive north of where we're sitting.

"The settlers and soldiers thought that Native Americans attacked only in small war parties, making raids on lonely cabins and traveling settlers. Of course there were such raids right around here, as you probably know. Scalpings, even. The people who built your house would have known some of the victims.

"But no one imagined, back then, that the various tribes could gather together to form an organized army, let alone attack a U.S. Army camp.

"In 1791, President George Washington ordered General Arthur St. Clair to march north from Cincinnati with his troops, confront the Native forces wherever he found them, and end 'the Indian problem' once and for all.

"General St. Clair was ill at the time and had to be carried on a litter. His army numbered less than a thousand, smaller than he wanted. There were too few veterans and too many inexperienced recruits. Their guns were old, their hardtack, beans and rice were moldy, and a crook had sold them boxes of sand labeled 'gunpowder.' Some things never change.

"The army was outfitted with summer uniforms, but they didn't march until autumn and the nights were cold. There was no road north. They slashed their way through the woods, cutting a wide trail as they went. Men were quitting every day, sneaking off to return home.

"What they never dreamed was that members of the Miami, Wyandot, Seneca, Ottawa, Shawnee, Delaware, Chippewa and Potawatomi tribes had all contributed their best warriors to form an army of their own, about fourteen hundred strong, to deal with St. Clair's force.

"The leaders of the Native American forces were the best they had, and their names are famous, even today. The Shawnee chieftain Black Hoof was there with his war chief Weyapier-senwah, which means 'Blue Jacket' in Shawnee. Tarhe the Crane of the Wyandots and Simon Girty of the Senecas were present as well as a twenty-one-year-old scout who was destined to become his people's most famous leader in the years ahead. His name was Tecumseh, Shawnee for both 'Crouching Panther' and 'Shooting Star.' Perhaps the greatest Indian leader there that day was Little Turtle of the Miami tribe. His people called him 'Mihšihkinaahkwa,' which means 'Wise, with a soul of fire.'

"As St. Clair's shrinking army made its way north, the Indians followed, watched and waited.

"St. Clair made a fatal mistake. After making camp, he sent his best scouts off to try to capture Indians for questioning. But about sixty of them sneaked off to go back to their homes in Kentucky. To round them up, St. Clair sent three hundred of his bravest and best fighters after them.

"When the Indian scouts reported that St. Clair was now badly undermanned, Little Turtle and Blue Jacket both knew the time had come to take bold action.

"Little Turtle and Blue Jacket did not get along. They argued over which one should lead the army, and they still hadn't settled on whom it would be. Nonetheless, they put their heads together and settled on a brilliant plan. They divided their force into seventy squads of twenty warriors each. These squads formed a tight circle around St. Clair's camp.

"The attack came at dawn. Indians swept in simultaneously from three sides. Their orders were to kill the artillerymen immediately. As a result, only two cannon shots were fired during the entire battle.

"St. Clair was almost too sick to stand. He struggled onto a horse, but it was quickly shot from under him. He crawled around on the ground, frantically shouting orders. Soon St. Clair's second in command, General Richard Butler (after whom Butler County is named), was dead, along with most of the other officers. Three more horses were shot from under St. Clair later that day, and eight bullets ripped through his coat, but none found their mark, and incredibly, St. Clair's life was spared.

"The Americans tried to break out of the circle of Indians surrounding them. The braves repeatedly feinted back but held firm. After two and a half hours, the soldiers under Colonel William Darke (Darke County is named after him), using bayonets and swords, slashed open an escape route to the newly cut wilderness road, followed by St. Clair and whoever else could run, walk, or crawl. By then, however, the slaughter was over: only twenty-four Americans left the battlefield unharmed.

"The Natives could have easily chased after the escaping soldiers and killed them all. Blue Jacket favored the idea, but Little Turtle refused. He said it was enough that nearly a thousand U.S. soldiers were dead as well as many women and children camp followers. The Natives lost only about sixty warriors, an incredible difference.

"More American soldiers were killed that day than in any of George Washington's battles of the Revolutionary War.

"The leaders of the tribes were proud of their victory but wondered what the Americans had learned. They had their doubts as to whether the Americans would now honor their treaties and keep out of the tribes' ancestral lands.

"That lesson, of course, was *not* learned. What the Americans learned from St. Clair's defeat was not to repeat the same tactical mistakes. About three years later, another American army under General 'Mad Anthony' Wayne met the Indians at the Battle of Fallen Timbers and soundly defeated them. That battle and the Treaty of Greenville pretty much ended the future of Indians on their native soil in Ohio. They were all forced to move west, and not for the last time.

"Americans like to believe that only the Indians were cruel. Most people today vaguely remember stories of Indians torturing their captives to death. Certainly there was some of that. But plenty of horrific things were done by the white settlers and soldiers as well. Our soldiers would mutilate the wounded and even the dead who lay on the battlefield after combat.

"The Indians greatly feared having their dead mutilated because of their spirits. They wanted their dead buried honorably with their bodies intact. But Americans had even been known to dig up buried Indian corpses and desecrate them in all kinds of ways. Putting heads on poles and making grisly souvenirs out of body parts. Things like that.

"So a curious new custom arose among the Indians. They would go through all the motions of burying a chieftain beneath a marked gravestone, only to exhume the body later and bury it again in an undisclosed location marked by something like an unusual rock, but with no indication of who was buried there.

"For example, when Little Turtle died in Indiana, it appeared that he was buried there, but his body was actually removed and interred in Ohio near Chillicothe, where he was born.

"When Tecumseh, the last and greatest leader of the Shawnee, learned that Weyapiersenwah had died in Michigan, he led a party of mourning warriors to retrieve his body. After setting up a mock gravestone where Weyapiersenwah had fallen, Tecumseh brought the remains back to the area where the fallen hero had been born and passed his boyhood, somewhere north of present-day Mt. Vernon and south of Mansfield, not far from a settlement by the name of Bellville.

"Tecumseh had seen more of this continent than almost any other American of his time, having visited nearly all of the Native American tribes in an attempt to weave them into a single united force against the invading soldiers and settlers.

"Tecumseh felt that the grave of Weyapiersenwah warranted a special stone marker, and from his travels he recalled a stunning blue rock in the possession of the Chippewa Ojibwe who lived on the northern shores of Lake Superior.

"Given Weyapiersenwah's name – remember, it meant 'Blue Jacket' in Shawnee – Tecumseh resolved to secure from the Ojibwe the blue rock he remembered. It took some doing, but Tecumseh convinced the Ojibwe. He and his traveling company oomphed the blue rock and the body of Weyapiersenwah to the peaceful center of a large forest in north-central Ohio. There they lay Blue Jacket in his final resting place, leaving only the unmarked blue rock to mark the spot.

"A few years later, Tecumseh's body disappeared in a similar fashion after he was killed in the Battle of the Thames during the War of 1812. No one knows today where Tecumseh was buried.

"As for Weyapiersenwah, the location of his bones has never been known for sure either. Until now. Maybe."

7

Frontier Dentistry

"HELLO, Mr. Sowash."

"Hello, Dr. Woehrman."

"Climb onto the chair and lean back. There you go. How are you?"

"Aside from my dental issues?"

The doctor chuckled. "Yes, aside from those, which we'll take care of for you today. You're always up to something interesting. Tell me what thoughts are bumping around in your head these days. Here, let me adjust your bib."

"Well, it might sound strange, but I've been thinking a lot about a mysterious blue rock I found in the center of a big woods back when we still lived up home in north-central Ohio. I brought it with me when we moved down here to Cincinnati. I thought maybe you might be able to tell me what it is, where it came from and how it came to be where I found it in the forest."

"Me? I'm a dentist. What makes you think I could tell you anything about a blue rock you found?"

"Because just about every person to whom I mention this blue rock seems to know everything about it."

"Is that right? Open wide, please. You say it was blue. Did it have holes of various sizes drilled into it?"

"Uh-huh."

"This is going to sting just a little. It's funny you should ask me, but as a matter of fact I'm pretty sure I can tell you precisely what that rock is, where it came from and how it came to be abandoned in the woods.

"I don't know what you know about the history of dental medicine and practice in the United States. Most people don't know much. It's been a hobby of mine, and I've read just about everything ever written on the subject.

"The greatest hero of American dental history and the founder of dental education here is Dr. John Harris, the most famous native son of Pompey, New York. Take a sip, slosh it around and spit.

"He came west from New York on the Erie Canal in the mid-1820s and set up practice as a medical doctor in Madison, Ohio. From the start, he took a particular interest in dentistry.

Nowadays people take dental health pretty seriously. They know how to take care of their teeth. When they need some care, there's always a dentist a short drive away, right?"

"Ungha," I mumbled.

"But back then, there were no dentists in the modern sense of the word. People would damage their teeth eating hardtack, beans and rice, but they could not get care as we know it today. In fact, barbers made a side business of pulling teeth, and it makes me shudder to think of it. They just grabbed a pair of pliers and yanked. They had no concept of germs, and the only pain relievers they could offer were hard cider or corn whiskey.

"Unsurprisingly, people's teeth went bad a lot more often than they do today. Toothbrushes back then were made of hog bristles or even horsehair, and floss was unheard of.

"After learning all he could about the teeth and jaws of human beings, Dr. Harris moved to Bainbridge, Ohio and opened the first school of dentistry in America in 1827. OK, rinse out again and spit.

"You've written books about Ohio, and you've traveled the state. You must have seen the sign at the edge of Bainbridge, "Site of the First Dental College in America." Did you ever wonder why Dr. John Harris chose Bainbridge as the location for his school?"

"Unga-hunga."

"The clue is in the name: Bainbridge. In French, the word *bain* means 'bath.' You've probably heard of soapstone. The French call it *pierre de bain*. It is rather soft, usually grayish or bluish in color, and it is relatively easy to carve. For centuries, large slabs of *pierre de bain* or 'bath-stone' were carved into bathtubs for the aristocracy in France. Holding a smaller piece in your hand, it looks a little like a bar of soap. That's how it came to be known as 'soapstone' in English.

"Near Bainbridge there is a large soapstone quarry, and the town is named after the first bridge that was built there, spanning Paint Creek, just north of the village. You get to it by driving north from the center of the village on Quarry Street. Yes, they built the bridge using the local soapstone, or *pierre de bain* if you prefer, and there you have the origin of the village's name. At first, they called the town 'Pierre de Bain Bridge.' But people kept wondering, 'Who is this Pierre guy?' They couldn't grasp that *pierre* is simply French for 'rock.' So the name of the village was shortened to Bainbridge. Turn your head a little to the left.

"Now why do you suppose Dr. Harris wanted to locate his dental school near a soapstone quarry? Don't answer. Just keep your mouth open. I'll answer my own question. Because, back in those days, soapstone being easy to carve, doctors would fashion false teeth from the stuff. The density of soapstone is actually very close to the density of human teeth. As long as patients didn't mind having a bluish or grayish tooth in their dentures, the chips of soapstone could be glued to a base and would work fairly well.

"Also, soapstone was the perfect substance on which dental apprentices could practice drilling. Anyone can drill a rough hole in a piece of wood, but a dentist needs to acquire a steady hand before he's ready to make precise holes in teeth, and that takes practice. Also, 19th century drills obviously weren't electrically powered. To operate a drill, old-time dentists used a treadle device, the same kind that powered old-fashioned sewing machines. The dentist had to push his foot up and down at the same time he was drilling. It was like patting your head while rubbing your tummy, a skill unto itself that demanded a considerable amount of practice to master.

"Of course, beginners couldn't practice on humans. Then as now, dentists wanted their patients to be pleased with their work. So what you do you think they practiced on?"

"Hoaf-hone."

"Right.

"All this is explained at the Dr. John Harris Dental Museum in Bainbridge. It's a fascinating place and you ought to check it out. It's filled with objects that relate the history of dental progress, and it shows just how far dentistry has come since the days when Dr. Harris opened his school. They have a vast array of historical dental implements on display there. You really must go there to believe it. Rinse and spit.

"Truth is, Dr. Harris taught general medicine in his school, but with a specialty in dental work. His advertisements in the newspapers of the day can be seen at the museum, emphasizing his interest in dentistry, the specialty he favored in both practice and instruction.

"Dr. Harris also taught dental hygiene, particularly the virtues of flossing. Between the toes as well as the teeth, since podiatric hygiene is important, too. Dr. Harris always recommended flossing the teeth first and the toes afterward – not the other way around. Just kidding. That's an old dentist's joke."

"Mphm, mphm, mphm!"

"You don't have to laugh. Dr. Harris's school was short-lived, though. By 1830 he had moved to Chillicothe, abandoning his practice and leaving behind a group of nine disciples. Although small, this group was hugely important to the future of dental education. Two of the students went on to form the first two dental colleges in the United States: the Baltimore College of Dental Surgery, which opened in 1840, and the Ohio College of Dental Surgery, which was established in Cincinnati – I'm proud to say – in 1845.

"Dr. Harris' other seven students became itinerant dentists, traveling by covered wagon and on horseback. They made the rounds of the settlements of Ohio, Indiana and Kentucky, carrying a cargo that included a treadle-powered drill and various picks, pliers, and other tools. They also oomphed along with them a slab of soapstone on which to practice not only their drilling technique but also chipping, carving, shaving and polishing false teeth to be glued into a denture plate.

"As these pioneer dentists prospered, they were able to procure ivory and even the teeth of hippopotami, less and less expensively. These proved more suitable for false teeth than soapstone. And one last rinse-and-spit, please.

"How did I do? Pretty good? Glad to know it. The stone you found was almost certainly once the property of a wandering frontier dentist. When he realized that he could afford to buy ivory, he lightened his load by tossing out his practice soapstone, and that is how it came to be lying there on the forest floor when you came upon it. You can settle up with Dolores at the front desk."

8

Louis Bromfield

"YOU SAY YOU LIVED IN BELLVILLE for twelve years?"

"That's right. Jo was born and reared there. I was born and reared in Mansfield, ten miles north. Both our families were in Richland County for at least a half-dozen generations before we were born. After we got married, our first home was in Bellville. In those days, people got married first and then lived together instead of the other way around."

"Did you ever become acquainted with any Oysters?"

"Not really, but there are a lot of Oysters in Bellville; it's one of the old Bellville family names. The Bellville cemetery is full of Oysters, a claim few inland villages can make."

"You never made the acquaintance of Eureta Belle Oyster?"

"I heard her name around the village, but I don't think I ever met her. I think Jo's mother knew her. Why do you ask?"

Jerry Handwork, one of my friends from church, tilted his head quizzically, stroked his gray goatee, and stared at me over his thick round glasses for a time. "I'm asking about

Eureta Belle because her connection to your Blue Rock is as indisputable as it is amazing. I never dreamed I'd get to the bottom of this. Listen and mark me well. I can tell you some interesting things about the rock you found and brought here, things that are known to very, very few people."

I had entertained Jerry and his wife Paula with my tale of the Blue Rock while we'd sat over dessert around our dining table. We then adjourned to the pavilion in the upper garden and were sipping B&B, relishing our time together. Jerry is a man of letters, an ardent lover of nature, and a conservationist. He is a force to be reckoned with in the Cincinnati chapter of the Sierra Club.

Jerry is a Bromfield scholar, which is to say that he has made a deep study of the life and works of the Pulitzer Prize-winning Ohio author Louis Bromfield, who lived from 1896 to 1956.

Bromfield was born in my hometown of Mansfield, Ohio, so I considered myself more than usually aware of his life and work. I read all his books and often visited his famous Malabar Farm, now one of Ohio's finest state parks.

A bestselling novelist in the 1920s, Bromfield wrote many books that were made into successful Hollywood films, bringing him wealth and fame. He traveled the world and lived the glamorous life of an expat through the 1930s.

He had a home in the village of Senlis, north of Paris, where he hosted the literary luminaries of the day, including Gertrude Stein, Ernest Hemingway, and Scott Fitzgerald. He also chummed with Hollywood stars, such as Douglas Fairbanks, Leslie Howard, and later, Humphrey Bogart and

Lauren Bacall. It was said of Bromfield that he "collected people and noted their value the way some do with stamps."

Having grown up on a farm in Richland County, Bromfield was fascinated to learn the techniques of intensive gardening his neighbors in Senlis practiced. Bromfield's gardens at Senlis were greatly admired, even envied, by Gertrude Stein and her life-partner Alice B. Toklas. Among that couple's many dazzling acquaintances, the only friend who shared their passion for flowers and gardening was Louis Bromfield.

His fascination with gardens was also shared in his close friendship with Edith Wharton, another famous American author living in France, who designed formal gardens when she was not busy writing novels.

Bromfield married, fathered three daughters, and after moving to France, supposed that it would be his permanent home. The family had a good life there, but he was restless and traveled widely, especially in India.

He made two long trips to the Asian subcontinent. Between tiger hunts, he visited Sir Albert Howard's soil institute in the state of Indore where he learned the value of compost or "brown gold," as he later termed cow manure, greatly amusing the many American skeptics who assigned no value to "cow pies" and "road apples."

Jerry the Bromfield scholar then proceeded to convey what he knew about the Blue Rock. Once Jerry Handwork begins to expound, there is no stopping him, and I was mighty eager to learn. I let him hold forth uninterrupted.

"Bromfield visited Baroda City, present-day Vadodara, where he was the honored guest of the revered Maharajah, Sayaiirao Gaekwad III. Upon hearing the news that his evil predecessor had died, Gaekwad journeyed to Baroda on foot from Kavlana, three hundred miles away. His arrival at Baroda City was greeted with great fanfare and he presented himself to the public as a humble yet enlightened monarch, saying, 'I have come here to rule with compassion.'

"Gaekwad's predecessor had squandered the treasury, spending it on all sorts of preposterous and ostentatious follies. A bathtub made of solid gold, a rug made of pearls, a pair of ruby slippers. Paranoid, convinced that some of his courtiers were conspiring to assassinate him, he poisoned them with arsenic. When he died, no one mourned his passing.

"Fortunately for the people of Baroda, the new Maharajah made the welfare of his people his highest priority, both in word and deed, and came to be admired and loved to the point of reverence.

"Bromfield was fascinated by the traditional farming techniques of the peasants of India, who, having practiced agriculture for thousands of years on the same few acres, had learned how to replenish the soil. Gaekwad perceived the depth of Bromfield's interest and allowed Bromfield to stay for several months as his honored house guest.

"When Bromfield and his family announced that they would soon return to their home in France, Gaekwad presented his famous American friend with a worthy gift, a beautiful blue stone that had been discovered centuries before in the foothills of the

Himalayas. It had been among the treasures of the Baroda Maharajahs since time immemorial. The gold bathtub, the pearl rug, the ruby slippers were ridiculous. The blue rock was fabulous.

"Nowadays, one would hesitate to accept such a cumbersome gift because of the outrageous fees the airlines charge for extra cargo. But of course, Bromfield and his family had traveled by ship. So Bromfield gratefully accepted the gift and transported it, along with his family, his tiger skins, and his luggage, back to Senlis. He commissioned a French cabinet-maker to create a wooden pedestal for it in the elaborate decorative style of Louis XIV, and it graced the salon where he entertained his guests with drinks and stories.

"The time he passed in India enabled Bromfield to write his most critically acclaimed novel, *The Rains Came*, which was adapted into a blockbuster film starring Myrna Loy and Tyrone Power. Supervising the writing of the film script, he befriended both of those famous actors."

When Jerry Handwork paused to take a sip of B&B, I seized the opportunity to interrupt his discourse.

"I know a bit about Bromfield. As you may know, he is much better known, nowadays, in Europe than he is in America. When Jo and I toured France in 1994 with our two children, we stayed in Chamonix for two nights. We had hoped to ride the gondola up Mont Blanc, but it was 'socked in' with fog the whole time we were there.

"When we were checking in at our hotel, the gentleman at the reception counter noticed that our nine-year-old boy, Chappy, was completely absorbed in writing. In those days, stories just poured out of the little guy, and he wrote them down on a yellow notepad he always carried with him. The receptionist said to me, in French, 'Perhaps he will grow up to become a great American author like Ernest Hemingway or Louis Bromfield.' I was quick to say, with pride, that I had been born and raised in Mansfield, Louis Bromfield's hometown, and that I had visited his famous Malabar Farm on many occasions. I had even been to Senlis to see the house where he had lived as an expat. The Frenchman was delighted to hear this, and he immediately showed me into the guest library adjacent to the lobby. There on the shelves were at least twenty books by Bromfield, all of them in French translations."

Jerry nodded and said, "Yes." Much better at talking than at listening, he returned to his narrative.

"Bromfield made a fortune from *The Rains Came,* but it marked the end of his time in France. With war in Europe imminent, he sold his home in Senlis and returned to his home in Ohio. Itching to put into practice the farming techniques he had learned in France and India, he used the proceeds from *Rains* to buy four contiguous farms in southern Richland County and set about replenishing the soil.

"Farmed for a century, the land was exhausted and depleted. Combining them into a single piece of real estate, Bromfield named his holdings Malabar Farm, saying that 'nothing could be more appropriate than giving the farm an Indian name – because India made it possible.' He would always remind people that, second only to the hills of southern Richland County, the most beautiful place he had ever seen was the Malabar coast of India."

"I haven't seen the Malabar coast," I made bold to interject, "but I can vouch for the beauty of southern Richland County."

"Bromfield the writer and world traveler," my friend continued without comment, "reinvented himself as a farmer and became one of the earliest proponents of sustainable agriculture, what we would today call 'organic' farming. Malabar Farm was to serve as the laboratory where he would demonstrate the innovative (which in this case means 'ancient') farming techniques he had learned and experiment with new ones.

"Many farmers in the area scoffed at his newfangled notions about crop rotation and the like. One of them directed Bromfield's gaze to a hilltop pasture and told him to observe just how green the grass was. 'My family,' the farmer said, proudly, 'has grazed our cattle on that field for three generations, and the soil is just as fertile now as it was on Day One.'

'Not so!' Bromfield retorted. 'How could it be? Every head of cattle that your family shipped out for slaughter took along with it 700 pounds of nutrients that were never returned to the soil. Where do you think the bones and muscle of those bulls and cows came from in the first place? Right up out of the dirt. You've taken 100,000 pounds of nutrients from those fields and never replaced them. What you've got up there is a green desert.'

"He was right, of course, but you can imagine that his neighbors didn't all take kindly to his blunt remarks."

"No, I don't suppose they were plea—."

"Malabar Farm became, in the late 1940s and early '50s, the most famous farm in America. Bromfield did the lecture circuit, talking not about literature but about agriculture. And he wrote about agriculture, too. Some say his best writing is his non-fiction about Malabar Farm and the surrounding area known as Pleasant Valley.

"The *New Yorker* magazine once printed a whimsical poem by E.B. White that begins,

> Malabar Farm is the farm for me,
> It's the greenest farm in the whole count-ree.

"Bromfield wanted Malabar Farm to make people aware of the techniques that had enabled the farmers of India to grow crops on the same acres for thousands of years without depleting them and, at the same time, to be a celebration of the best of American agriculture. Accordingly, he had his 19-room farmhouse built in the best Greek Revival architectural tradition. It looks like a large-scale version of an 18th-century Connecticut farmhouse except for one exotic touch. In the center of the pediment above the white pillars of his entrance, Bromfield placed a statue of Ganesh, one of the best-known and most beloved gods of the Hindu religion.

"Oh, yes, Ganesh, the smiling elephant," I declared.

"Ganesh is easily recognized because atop his human body he has the head of a smiling elephant. He is revered as the remover of obstacles, the patron of arts and sciences, and the fount of human intellect and wisdom. He is the god of beginnings and, as such, he is invoked at the commencement of rites and ceremonies. A kind of Apollo figure, Ganesh is the patron saint of Indian literature and is believed to bless all who yearn for learning.

"Bromfield also brought to Malabar Farm the blue rock that had been given to him by Maharajah Gaekwad and the wooden Louis XIV display pedestal that had been made for it in France. Bromfield believed that the stone had brought him good luck, perhaps along with the blessings of Ganesh, and so he displayed the stone on its pedestal in the grandest of the bedrooms he maintained for his famous and colorful guests.

"To run the farm and its household, Bromfield hired a sizeable team of farm hands and house servants, including several members of the Oyster family, who live in nearby Lucas, Butler and Bellville. One of these was Eureta Belle Oyster, whom you said your mother-in-law knew."

"Yes, although I can't recall anything about her except the funny name."

"Eureta Belle became Bromfield's head housekeeper.

"Though Bromfield had spent a fortune on his venture, the crops and dairy operation at Malabar Farm never broke even, and some of Bromfield's experiments were costly but unsuccessful. To meet the costs of operating the farm, Bromfield earned extra income by lecturing far and wide. At home he wrote furiously, churning out books that were written too quickly. Not among his best, they did not sell very well. His popularity as a writer was fading and his bills were mounting. He was a proud man and kept up a show of success, but he was going ever deeper into debt.

"The most memorable event that ever took place at Malabar Farm was the wedding of Humphrey Bogart and Lauren Bacall. They were both friends of his, people Bromfield had 'collected' while in Hollywood. He was thrilled and honored when they accepted his invitation to be married and to honeymoon at Malabar Farm. There's a photograph of the three of them, smiling broadly, hovering round the wedding cake as Lauren does the slicing.

"Miss Eureta Belle Oyster, good of heart but cheated of feature, was never married, never asked. Like so many lonely women of her age in that time, she deeply, longingly cherished Humphrey Bogart, the one and only man in her life. She was an avid fan and eagerly attended all his films. She assiduously followed his doings as they were recounted in fan magazines. When Bogart left his second wife for the nineteen-year-old Lauren Bacall, Eureta Belle was at first devastatingly disappointed but then transported to even higher ecstasy. It was the most talked-about romance of the day.

"In 1945, upon learning that Bogart and Bacall were to be married at Malabar Farm, Miss Oyster's feelings of anticipation, half joy and half dread, were almost more than she could bear. She resolved that everything would be perfect at the house when they arrived and during their stay. Thoughts of dust preyed upon her rest. She went about her chores in a frenzy and bullied her assistants to outdo themselves in cleaning, sweeping, wiping, and dusting.

"When the famous couple pulled up in front of the farmhouse, Eureta Belle was on hand, along with Bromfield, his family and all his other employees, to give them a cheering welcome. Although Bogart was far shorter than she supposed from his movies, Eureta Belle nearly fainted with emotion when Bogie breezed past only a few feet away.

"Eureta Belle did not have occasion to speak with the couple except to murmur 'You're welcome' or 'My pleasure' when they thanked her for serving them. This was as it should be, she thought. She was a fan, but so were millions of other Americans, and she was certain that both stars had long since tired of strangers telling them how much their movies were admired. The respectful distance that she kept does her credit although in truth she really had nothing to say to impress either of them.

"After the happy couple departed, Eureta Belle relaxed the stringency she had imposed upon her staff. They kept the house clean, to be sure (or at least as clean as possible, considering that Bromfield gave his four active boxer dogs the run of the house), but Eureta Belle reserved to herself the cleaning of the 'honeymoon suite' where Bogart and Bacall had passed their wedding night.

"She changed the sheets and freshened the pillows with special care. The notion of the couple brushing their teeth over the sink in the bathroom or regarding themselves in the mirror made her heart hammer in her breast. She became dizzy when she envisioned them dressing and undressing in the suite. The very thought of them, embracing in that bed, languishing in one another's arms, thrilled Eureta Belle to a state of rapture that modern day nerve specialists have termed 'the heebie jeebies.'

"Eureta Belle acquired a very fine feather duster and used it exclusively for dusting the blue rock from India which sat on its pedestal in the nuptial bedroom. It gave her chills to reflect that the blue rock had been a mute witness as the couple had engaged, a few feet away, in sanctified 'oompus boompus.'

Dwelling on this made her lightheaded and caused her, on at least one occasion, to faint dead away.

"Meanwhile, Bromfield's literary career was faltering. Critics dismissed his later work as superficial and hastily written, though a few sold well on the coattails of his name.

"His financial situation worsened, the result of the high cost of maintaining his experimental farm and the money he lavished on famous and not-so-famous clingers-on who took advantage of his hospitality. He concocted various schemes to re-establish his fortune, raising capital to replicate Malabar in Texas and even Brazil. Financially, these came to naught.

"After his wife Mary died in 1952, Bromfield took up with the billionaire heiress Doris Duke, who genuinely shared his interest in horticulture. Eureta Belle Oyster did not approve. Eureta Belle was heard to sniff, 'You can lead a horticulture, but you can't make her think.'

"Then Bromfield's health began to deteriorate. A heavy drinker and smoker, he was diagnosed with cancer. His once robust good health and high spirits declined rapidly. When his medical care ate up his remaining capital and he could borrow no more, his last resort was to sell the forest of virgin timber that was the farm's crown jewel and, conservationist that he was, his pride and joy. The deal wasn't quite closed when he died in 1956.

When the farm was acquired by the state of Ohio to be developed into a state park, the precious forest was purchased and donated to the state by Doris Duke, for which action she is highly to be praised. Today it's known as the Doris Duke Woods and is one of the highlights of a visit to Malabar Farm.

"A month or so after Bromfield's death, his daughters announced 'the yard sale to end all yard sales.' Almost penniless, they intended to auction off all of their father's possessions.

"I kind of remember that," I said. "I'd have been eight years old."

"Eureta Belle, who was the last of the servants to be dismissed after Bromfield's passing, was aghast. She wished that she could purchase everything and donate the treasures to the state to be showcased in the Bromfield house, now part of the prospective state park. But her savings were meager. Still an ardent admirer of Bromfield and his legacy, she asked everyone she knew to attend the auction, buy a few items, and then donate them after the park became official. Many of her friends and family did this, and it is in no small part due to Eureta Belle's efforts that many of those furnishings are still on display today.

"She herself bid on only one object, the blue rock that had passively witnessed the Bogart/Bacall consummation. When the bidding reached $4.50, she blanched and resolved to bid only once more. Shouting through clenched teeth, she made heard her final bid of $5.00. That doesn't sound like much today, but it was a lot of money for an unemployed housekeeper living on hardtack, beans and rice. Her bid was successful, though to her lasting regret, the Louis XIV-style pedestal was beyond her means.

"Her brothers Dilbert and Detlef oomphed the blue rock into their pickup truck and transported it to Eureta Belle's little country cottage near Bellville. At her direction, the brothers placed it in the position of honor at the center of her garden.

"She planted the loveliest flowers she could find all around it and dusted it every day with her special feather duster. When Bogart died a year later, the blue rock became her private shrine to the late film idol.

"Eureta Belle's original intention, in all sincerity, was to return the blue rock to Malabar Farm after it opened as a state park. But when the park opened, she hesitated. 'Those park rangers won't know the blue rock from Adam,' she said to herself. 'They won't none of them tend to it the way I do.'

"After deciding not to return the rock, Eureta Belle began to fear for it. After Bogart's death it was clearly unthinkable to lose it. But what might happen? The park authorities might come round and try to buy it. She would refuse to sell, of course, but suppose they took some kind of legal action against her. Suppose they invoked eminent domain and sent the sheriff and a posse to return her precious blue rock to Malabar Farm. The thought became Eureta Belle's nightmare.

"That is why in late 1957 she coaxed Dilbert and Detlef to remove the blue rock from its place of honor in her garden. When she told the brothers that she had found a spot for the blue rock 'way back in the woods' behind her place, they thought their sister was half-crazy, and maybe she was. But they loved her, and they knew that once Eureta Belle had her mind set on something there was no use in trying to talk her out of it. So the brothers moved the blue rock to the very spot in the woods where you found it resting many years later.

"The beautiful flowers Eureta Belle had grown around the blue rock when it adorned her garden would not thrive in the deep shade of the dark forest. So she planted daffodil bulbs, hosta, and ferns that would come up every year, long after she was gone. Every May she planted annuals as well. She favored the flowers known as impatiens, which provided a cheery display of pure white and bright red which she thought appropriate. For her, the white impatiens symbolized the purity of Miss Bacall on her wedding night and the red ones did the same for the understated passion of the great Bogart, who would have been, she imagined, a little detached, even on his wedding night.

"Each year on January 14, the anniversary of Bogart's death, Eureta Belle purchased fresh flowers from the flower shop in Bellville and made her way through the snowy forest to the shrine she had created. After brushing away the snow, she communed with the rock, reciting aloud a litany of her own invention, naming all of Bogart's seventy-five feature films in the order of their release, beginning, appropriately, with *A Devil with Women* and ending, aptly, with *The Harder They Fall*. Each time when she came to *The African Queen*, she would pause and sigh deeply before continuing. Upon finishing her litany, she knelt before the stone and, after kissing it warmly but reverentially, she proffered her heartfelt gratitude to the Deity that such a beautiful creature as Bogart had briefly graced God's green earth."

At last Jerry Handwork ceased to speak. Almost. He lifted his glass of B&B saying, "Here's to Eureta Belle Oyster!" I joined him in the toast.

9

The Reverend Rutherford B. Hayes Prindle

ALMOST EVERY SUNDAY there are new faces at the worship service at my church, Mt. Auburn Presbyterian. After the service, I try to make a point of greeting them, learning their names and asking them to linger for a bit at the "coffee hour" in the church's Social Hall.

Responding to my greeting, one lady who was about my age said, "It's our first time at your church. We're just passing through Ohio seeing old friends and family and then we'll head back to Atlanta."

"So you're originally from Ohio?"

"Oh, yes."

"Where exactly?"

"It's just a little crossroads in north-central Ohio. No one has ever heard of it."

"North-central Ohio? I'm from Richland County. Try me."

"Richland County? Well, I grew up in the country between Palmyra and Ankenytown."

"How about that! I grew up in Mansfield and my wife is from Bellville, where we lived for twelve years. What church did you go to?"

"Oh, just a little country church. My family attended 'The Watch Your Step Church of the Eager Believers.'"

"So you grew up an 'Eager Beaver?'"

"Yes, that's what the other folks around those parts used to call us," she said with a smile. "Do you know where the church is?"

"I certainly do. Is it still a going concern?"

"No, I'm sorry to say. We were just up there, and its day has come and gone. But while it was going, it was going strong, and there were a lot of good people there. We weren't exactly Holy Rollers, more like Pentecostals, though that description Isn't really accurate either. We were never affiliated with any other churches. We were totally independent, and the Eager Believers pretty much figured out for themselves what they believed in and what they didn't.

"Of course, the pastor had a lot to do with that. The most colorful pastor we ever had was the Reverend Rutherford B. Hayes Prindle."

"I remember people talking about him. Wasn't he also an inventor?"

"He was an inventor, a mechanic, a scholar of the Bible, an herbalist and the best mushroom hunter in north-central Ohio. He would show up at church on Sundays in May with bushels of them and send every family home with a paper sack full. Roll 'em in flour and fry 'em up in butter and—"

"Oh, I know! There's no better flavor in the world. People in Cincinnati don't know anything about forest mushrooms. They don't seem to grow this far south."

"And he was a collector of relics, too, though that got to be something of an embarrassment, at least for some people."

"How so?"

"Well, it started the first time he went to visit the Holy Land. The congregation chipped in and raised just enough for him to make the trip. He had to leave Mrs. Prindle behind, but that was just as well as she couldn't swim and had a fear of traveling by ship. This was back in the late '40s when traveling by air was something only rich people did. I was a little girl at the time. We had 'supply preachers' while he was gone, and I remember how strange it was to see someone else in the pulpit other than Reverend Prindle. He was a fixture.

"The first Sunday after he came back was a big occasion. We always had a church picnic on the last Sunday of August, right after church, and it was our biggest social of the year. People came from all around and far away. You'd see people there that you never saw at any other time. And the food? Oh, my. We didn't eat hardtack, beans and rice, I can tell you that! There was fried chicken, meat loaf, green bean casserole, macaroni and cheese, potato salad, homemade pickles, and a lot else. And the best pies ever. All kinds. Every kind imaginable. Even elderberry pie, which I've never tasted anywhere else.

"Well, Pastor Prindle made sure to come back from his trip to the Holy Land in time for the annual picnic. They set up tables and chairs in the shade of the great big trees in what we called 'the backyard' of the church. There was an outhouse there and lots of picnic tables. But we needed 'way more than just the picnic tables to seat all those people, so everybody brought card tables and folding chairs from home.

"After everybody ate all they could, there were still twelve bushels of food left over, like when Jesus fed the five thousand. But nobody was in a hurry to leave. We all wanted to hear about Pastor Prindle's trip, and he really wanted to tell us. He made a fine speech about it and described the sacred sites he had visited. Few of us had ever been farther away than Columbus or Cleveland, so everyone listened very carefully to all he had to say. He was a fine preacher and knew how to put pictures in your head.

"Then he said he'd made a purchase. He paused, and after a moment, he very dramatically reached in his pocket and pulled out a large, dark brown splinter of wood, about a half inch wide and about eight inches long. He said it was a splinter from one of the boards from Noah's ark.

"We were hushed in awe. He said that there were shops in Jerusalem that sold all kinds of things like this and that it had cost a pretty penny, but that if it inspired folks to walk humbly with God then it was worth it. Being a little girl, I bought that story – hook, line, and sinker. I was very surprised, even I would say a little shocked, when I heard my father say that it couldn't be real, a waste of good money. He said Reverend Prindle had let someone sell him 'a pig in a poke.' My mother shushed him, but I had the feeling she agreed. Pastor Prindle built a display case with a glass top and put the splinter in it with a label telling all about it. It sat just to the right as you entered the church.

"Three years later, the Reverend went to visit the Holy Land a second time. This time he brought back a dusty red brick that he said came from the pile of rubble after the walls of Jericho came a-tumblin' down. I believed it was true. We were the Eager Believers, and none was more eager than me.

"Well, he went back to the Holy Land about every three years from then on. I remember in my teens, he brought back a stone from the Tower of Babel, the sling that David used to fling the stone that brought down Goliath, and one of the ankle bones that had been connected to the foot bone and the leg bone when Ezekiel saw all those bones in the desert come rattling back together into skeletons. All these things were placed in the display case with little labels.

"By now I was eighteen and beginning to have my doubts, though I was careful not to put them into words when I was with other Eager Believers.

"All along Pastor Prindle kept coming up with inventions, too, and he would unveil one of them each year at the church picnic. Folks came to expect it of him, and we'd have been disappointed if he had failed to show us something new and amazing.

"He invented a chewing gum locker that you could wear on a chain around your neck to keep your chewing gum fresh. He invented a pair of pajamas for an infant made out of an old mop, so that as the child crawled around it would clean the floor. He invented an upside-down half-umbrella that men could attach to their suspenders to catch the whiskers when they trimmed their beards and mustaches. A right-side-up umbrella attached to a special harness for dogs to wear when their owners walked them on rainy days. A miniature one-piece shirt-and-pants combination swimsuit and bathing cap made of cork to keep babies afloat in the bathtub. A miniature hammock that Reverend Prindle announced as the world's first truly comfortable bicycle seat. I don't know why that one never caught on.

"Pastor Prindle made what turned out to be his final trip to the Holy Land during the summer after I graduated from high school. That year's picnic was one that nobody will ever forget. During the entire year before his last trip, he spread the word that he was at work on his greatest invention, but he wouldn't tell anybody what it was.

"When he got back, we had the annual church picnic in the church's 'backyard' next to the woods, as always. But this time, when we went out there, right in the center of the ring of picnic tables there were two strange things hidden under covers. The smaller one was underneath a tablecloth, and the larger one, which was about as big as one of the picnic tables, was under a couple of quilts.

"After everybody had eaten all they could hold, Reverend Prindle made his usual speech about the things he had seen in the Holy Land. Then he gestured toward the smaller concealed object, the one under the tablecloth. He said he had brought back something very, very special and that, before he showed it to us, he wanted us to listen to the Word of God. He had memorized most of the Bible.

"Now he recited:

> And Jacob went out from Beersheba, and went
> toward Haran. And he lighted upon a certain
> place, and tarried there all night, because the sun
> was set; and he took of the stones of that place,
> and put them for his pillows, and lay down in that
> place to sleep. And he dreamed, and behold a
> ladder set up on the earth, and the top of it
> reached to heaven: and behold the angels of God
> ascending and descending on it.

"What he had brought home, he explained, was the actual
stone on which that patriarch had pillowed his head on that one
occasion back in olden times and that, now, it was underneath
this tablecloth.

"With that, he pulled the tablecloth aside and there it was, a
beautiful blue stone, blue as the sky but with a little white mixed
in. It was the prettiest thing any of us had ever seen. I could see
how it was the sort of stone Jacob would use for a pillow, though
pretty as it was, it was still a rock and couldn't have been very
comfortable to sleep on.

"Then Reverend Prindle said that he was ready to share with
the world his greatest invention and that, in a way he could not
have foreseen, it had to do with Jacob's pillow. He reminded us
that the ways of the Lord are mysterious.

"He pulled the quilts aside and revealed something the likes
of which none of us had ever seen. It was a chair, that much was
plain to see. You sat on it. But it was nailed down onto a little
square platform that had what looked to be the tracks of a small

tank mounted on both the right and left sides. It had a steering wheel, too. Everybody wondered, what could it be?

"Reverend Prindle said that it was a wheelchair that could go places other wheelchairs can't go. Suppose someone in a wheelchair wanted to go into the woods to hunt mushrooms or gather herbs. He said the thing could go up and down even the steepest of hillsides and that it could be steered around trees and boulders and go right over holes and ditches.

"Then he declared that Jacob's pillow was not a thing to be kept inside a display case. It was a thing of Nature, a thing of God's Creation and, just as Jacob had found it in the wilderness halfway between Beersheba and Haran, so we must now place it in the closest thing we had to a wilderness, halfway between Palmyra and Ankenytown.

"With that, he and two or three of the church men placed Jacob's pillow onto the seat of the chair in the center of his contraption, pointed the machine toward the woods and fired up the engine by yanking on a cord, the way you would start a lawnmower. The thing putted slowly along, and everybody followed. The pastor walked alongside, his hand on the steering wheel. When it entered the woods, it just kept on going, pushing right over the honeysuckle and crushing the ferns. When it was heading straight toward a big old tree, Reverend Prindle would nudge the steering wheel and it would go around the tree.

"The Reverend was getting on in years by that time, and he huffed and puffed, keeping up with the thing as it went along, puffing especially hard going uphill. It rumbled along for about an hour until it reached a place that Pastor Prindle declared was the place the Lord had chosen as the perfect American location for Jacob's pillow.

"He stopped the engine, and he and his helpers oomphed the blue rock off the chair and laid it on the forest floor.

"Then he proclaimed, in a loud voice, that just as Jacob had laid his head on this pillow and been granted a vision of the connection between Heaven and Earth, so, also, in our time and place – and here he quoted Scripture again:

> And it shall come to pass in the last days, I will pour out of my Spirit upon all flesh: and your sons and your daughters shall prophesy, and your young men shall see visions, and your old men shall dream dreams.

"Then he prayed a prayer of thanksgiving for the goodness of God, and at the end he prayed that God would keep Jacob's blue 'bedrock' in the memories of all of us and be an inspiration to us forever. He said 'Amen,' fired up the wheelchair again, climbed on, and we all followed back to the church. That was a day to remember."

10

Contraband

IT WAS A DARK and stormy night. Well, a snowy night. The Ohio Valley was buried beneath two feet of the stuff and still it fell. I felt sorry for travelers. As for Jo and myself, we were snug and happy.

On such nights I think of the lines Shakespeare gives to Touchstone in *As You Like It*: "When I was at home I was in a better place: but travellers must be content."

I looked out the window and watched snowflakes the size of moths slanting downwards beneath the streetlights. The phone rang.

"A friend in need is a friend indeed," said a familiar voice.

"Dirck Philby, is that you?" said I.

"It is indeed. How are you?"

"Full of piss and vinegar and greatly enjoying the snowstorm."

"Alas, not we. Sandra and I were in Louisville to see a matinee performance at the Players Theatre, and we hoped to make it back home to Wooster tonight, but 'man proposes and a storm disposes.' We've been creeping along at twenty for three hours and all the motels are full. We're out on I-275 about twenty minutes from your place. Could we impose upon you?"

"Impose? To host you and Sandra? Nothing would tickle us more pinkly."

An hour later the four of us were sitting by the fireplace in the living room, toasty warm and delighting one another with travel tales. The fire's reflected flames danced in our spectacles and off the shiny top of Dirck's bald head. Drambuie, "the oil of conversation," worked its magic.

"Of all my journeys," Dirck said at length, "surely the most exciting was my one and only flight in a hot air balloon. And even then, it wasn't so much the flight itself that was exciting as the story the pilot told me. It takes a deal of telling but we're in no hurry and I think you'll find it worth your time to hear it."

"Pray, continue!" I said.

"Ever since my boyhood days, I was fascinated by hot air balloons. I read *The Mysterious Island* and *In Search of the Castaways* and *The Twenty-One Balloons*. I read about the Montgolfier Brothers who invented the hot air balloon and of Auguste Piccard and his pioneering stratospheric research flights. I dreamed of the day when I, too, would rise off the ground in a hot air balloon. When I was about twelve, I even tried to make one out of sheets and a laundry basket, but it was beyond me.

"About ten or twelve Christmases back my dear Sandra presented me with a gift certificate, good for one ascent in a hot air balloon to be scheduled sometime during the following summer. How exciting!

"One summer evening six months later the phone rang. It was Todd Carpenter, pilot and sole proprietor of the Archimedes Hot Air Balloon Transport Company.

"'The weather looks good for a flight tomorrow morning. Are you available?' asked Todd.

"I assured him that I was, and we agreed to meet at 6 a.m. in a field near the intersection of two township roads in the rural area of Wayne County, out near Chesterville.

"Sandra and Christopher, who was about twelve at that time, got up with me at the crack of dawn and we made our way into the depths of Amish Country.

"There was Todd, as promised, at the appointed time and place. He had already spread out the cloth balloon in a grassy field and laid the basket on its side. He greeted us with a confident smile and invited Christopher to hold up the balloon's opening and to position it to receive hot air from his propane burner. It was loud and gusty and soon the balloon began to fill, to writhe, to stretch like a waking giant.

Todd's wife was helping with the preparations as well. Todd explained that she would be following us in their van to be there when we landed. He said Sandra and Christopher could follow her in our car so that they could be waiting, too. As the balloon rose and filled, it lifted the basket to an upright position and the ropes attaching the basket to the balloon grew taut.

"'All aboard!' yelled Todd, and we both clambered in.

"The basket was still firmly on the ground and Sandra and Christopher were right in front of me. I looked straight into Sandra's eyes. She said, 'Are you excited?' I said, 'You bet I am!'

"'Kiss 'em goodbye!' said Todd.

"I did, and I thought they both looked just a little bit worried. I felt a little badly about giving them cause to worry, but I guess I'd prefer to have them be a little worried at such a moment as opposed to their not being worried at all.

"'Up we go!' Todd blasted more of the propane's flame into the balloon.

"The burner, about the size and shape of a large fire extinguisher, emitted a bright flame, mostly reddish and orange, blue on the upper edge. The balloon lifted gently off the ground and very quickly I found myself looking down onto the upturned faces of Sandra and Christopher, waving, just five feet below. Then ten feet. Then twenty.

"I looked around. It was a beautiful morning. A clear sky, fields and forests in all directions. I looked down again. There were our car and Todd's van. There were Sandra, Christopher and Todd's wife, still waving. I was still just close enough to make out the expressions on their faces. They were beaming.

"When I'd climbed into the basket, the top edge of it had seemed high, but now, looking down at my feet and then, a few inches away, a drop of a hundred feet to the ground, the basket seemed to come barely up to my waist. I clung tightly to the ropes. I gazed off in the distance for what seemed a short while, but when I looked down it took me a moment to find the field where the vehicles were. The fields spread in all directions, and the farmland below looked like a gigantic quilt made of green and beige squares and rectangles.

"Five minutes later, looking down, I could not discern the field from which we had ascended. The layout resembled a vast, zany chessboard stretching out in all directions.

"We floated over a farm house perhaps five hundred feet below and watched as a man stepped from his front porch into his yard. 'Hello!' he shouted, and I was surprised how clearly we could hear his voice. It made sense, there being nothing but thin air between him and us. 'Hello!' we shouted back. 'Hey, Martha,' he yelled, turning back toward his front door, 'there's a hot air balloon going over.' She came out and they both waved. 'Nice day for it!' she yelled. 'Glorious!' I yelled back.

"Sheep were afraid of us. When we approached the edge of a field, they fled in panic to the far side, and as we crossed over the field they would scurry to the opposite side, now behind us.

"Todd told me that pigs get very excited when they see a hot air balloon overhead. 'They plant one foot on the ground and run as hard as they can with the other three legs so that they spin in circles. It's a weird thing to see ten pigs spinning in circles as fast as they can go.' After he told me that, I hoped we would fly over some pigs, but we did not. For the sake of the porcine mental health of Wayne County, it was perhaps just as well.

"We talked, Todd and I. He confessed that hot air ballooning was an expensive hobby, and he could understand if some people thought it was foolhardy. 'But,' he said, 'I love it.'

"I asked him if he had had any adventures worth the telling. He said he'd managed to avoid storms and high winds. He said that more than once, passengers found that they just couldn't handle it, requiring a landing sooner than planned.

"Todd was quiet for a few moments. Then he said, 'The oddest thing of all happened just a few weeks ago. It should have been on the news, but the police said to keep it quiet, at least for now. I don't think they'd mind me telling you, though.'

"'I'm not only a balloon pilot,' said Todd. 'I couldn't make a living just doing that. I'm also a school teacher so I'm off for the summer. A couple of weeks ago the phone rang at home and I answered it.

"'"Ziss Todd Carpenter?" a man's voice asked.

"'"Yes."

"'"Archimedes Balloon Transport Company?"

"'"That's right."

"'"How much advance notice you need before a lift-off?"

"'"Um, well, I mean … at least forty-five minutes. But it also depends on the weather. Who is this, please?"

"'"Call me Smith. John Smith. What do you charge?"

"'"I told him."

"'"I'll pay you five times that much – in cash! – if you can be on standby and ready to take me up on short notice sometime

– I don't know how long – after noon tomorrow. Could be five minutes after noon, could be an hour or two or even three."

""""That's very generous of you, but I'll have to check the weather forecast."

""""The weather be damned," he said. "Don't screw around. I'm gonna tell you where we're gonna lift off from.   And when."

"'I probably should have hung up on him right there, but my finances were at a low ebb just then and, to tell the truth, I was intrigued.

"'He wanted me to lift off from behind some abandoned warehouses out in the country beyond town, over toward Smithville. He said to drive behind them and set up for the balloon launch out of sight from the road. He said to have everything ready at noon sharp, but that if he wasn't there I should wait until he arrived.

"'So, call me stupid, but I did just what he said to do, and at noon we had the balloon just about fully inflated and ready to rise. A car with tinted windows came roaring around the warehouses, spotted us, pulled up to where we were and stopped. A man jumped out, pulling after him a big black bowling bag that was coming apart at the seams. From the way he slung it out of the car, I could tell it was very heavy. He had barely slammed the door shut when the car roared off again.

"'He was wearing a black suit and sunglasses. He looked around in all directions and then noticed my wife.

""""Who's ziss?" he shouted, pointing at her.

""""My wife," I said.

""""She's outta here, right now!" he said. I nodded to Karen, who promptly got in our van and drove off.

"""The man looked around nervously and oomphed his heavy bowling bag up over the side of the basket and lowered it onto the basket's floor.

""""What's in the bag?" I asked.

""""Never you mind," he said. "Get us outta here, fast."

"""He climbed in before I could ask him to, and I climbed in too. I told him that his bag looked to be pretty heavy, and the basket was made only of wicker, but he didn't want to hear it. He seemed to be in a big hurry.

""""C'mon, c'mon, c'mon!" he said. He had a mean-looking mouth.

"""I sparked the burner and up we went. He watched very closely when I turned on the gas and used a hand-held candle-lighter to ignite the flame. Now, after looking around in all directions, he settled his gaze on a distant highway. Following his gaze, I saw three police cars, their lights flashing, speeding in the direction of the warehouse complex where we had lifted off.

""""What's going on here?" I asked him, politely. "Just get us outta here, fly-boy," he said.

"""My passenger looked straight up. "How long 'til we can get inside those clouds?" No passenger had ever asked me that before. "Ten, maybe fifteen minutes," I guessed. "Blow that torch again," he ordered. I obeyed.

"'Soon enough we were inside the cloud. Being inside a cloud is no different than driving a car through a thick fog except, of course, there's practically no danger of hitting a deer. "Ziss is good," he said when the fog had fully enveloped us. "Just stay inside the cloud."

"'We were in the fog for longer than I thought we would be. Maybe an hour. He was silent the whole time. Then the clouds lifted somewhat, and we could see farms and fields below again.

"""Where are we?" he asked.

"""Over Ashland County, about halfway between Ashland and Loudonville."

"""Where we headed?"

"""Richland County."

"""Don't give me this County talk. What towns are we near?"

"""Mansfield is off toward the northwest but we're heading southwest. We'll probably be in the vicinity of Lucas soon and then Butler and then Bellville. There's the Clear Fork Reservoir over there."

"""Find the biggest woods around and tell me when we're exactly over the middle of it."

""""Okay," I said. Another half hour of silence ensued. "See those woods down there?" I asked. "It's got to be the biggest woodland in southern Richland County." He nodded.

"'Just as we were floating over the center of the woods, he suddenly stooped and picked up his bowling bag. To the surprise of both of us, the side of it ripped open and a blue and white stone bumped out onto the floor of the basket. I winced when the basket made an ominous creaking, stretching noise.

""""What's that?" I asked.

""""What's what? You didn't see nothin.'"

"'"He bent over and lifted the stone. It was obviously very heavy. I didn't immediately realize what he was going to do. Then, to my horror, I did. He was oomphing it up high enough to drop it over the side. "You can't do that!" I shouted. "You're throwing too much weight overboard!" But it was too late. The instant he let go of the stone, the balloon shot upward like a rocket, maybe fifty miles per hour, going up a thousand feet before I could vent it. I've never experienced that before or since. It scared the bejesus out of me.

"'I'm not stupid. By now I was figuring things out. He was a thief and he had stolen a precious stone, maybe from a jeweler. He wanted to hide the evidence by dropping it into the middle of a woods where it would be lying, undiscovered, when he came back for it.

""""My God, man," I said. "You don't just drop that much weight all at once."

""""Relax," he said. "It's called ballast."

""""Yeah, I know what it's called. I carry ballast in these bags around the edge of the basket. They're filled with hardtack, beans and rice."

""""What?"

""""You can't just drop a sack of gravel. It might hurt someone when it falls. You have to think of that. This ballast is edible by wild animals, so it's ecologically sound. And if I ever get stranded somewhere, I can survive by eating it myself."

""""You're crazy," he said.

"""We were in a thick cloud once again.

"""He said, "Time to land this rig."

"""I looked at him. "You can't just land anywhere," I said. "There's electrical wires and trees and highways to consider."

""""The thing ain't gonna be down for long. Just land it." He pointed to his coat pocket. It bulged.

"""I gulped. Call me an idiot, but up 'til then, I hadn't been really scared.

""""Show me how to make this rig go down," he said. I showed him.

"""As we approached the ground, I gave him the same warning I give all my passengers. I said, "I have to tell you what's going to happen. It will feel like we're floating down like a feather, but don't be fooled. We're dropping faster than you think. When we're about ten feet from the ground it's going to feel like the earth shoots up at you like a fist and smacks you, HARD! So bend your knees, hang on to the ropes as tight as you can with both hands, and get ready for the shock. And we'll bounce up and down at least three or four times, so be ready for that, too."

"'He did as I had instructed. After the fourth bounce, the basket settled onto the ground. We were in a field of soy beans.

""'Now get out," he said. "All by your lonesome."

""'When one of us gets out, it's going to be like dumping two hundred pounds of ballast. She's going to shoot right up into the air again."

""'That's the general idea," he said, indicating his bulging pocket again.

""'You're going to leave me here," I said.

""'Yep." He handed me a thick envelope, filled with cash. "You done what you were told. Now get out."

""'I don't like the look of the weather," I said. The clouds were graying and a wind out of the southwest was kicking up. It smelled like rain.

""'That's not your problem," he said.

"'I got out and watched as my balloon leapt up again. I heard him fire up the burner and the balloon rose even faster.

"'I thought I'd never see my balloon again. A ten-thousand-dollar investment up in smoke … or hot air, as the case may be.

"'A week later, it turned up. The US Coast Guard found it, empty, in the middle of Lake Erie.'"

11

The Blue Blarney Stone

I LIKE TO DESCRIBE the acres that stretch away from behind our house, extending more than a mile to the Little Miami River, as a "greensward."

In fact it is a greensward, but a fuller account must mention that it is a public golf course operated and maintained by the Hamilton County Park Board. We often find golf balls lying in our gardens and coming upon them among the flowers and shrubs is almost as much fun as finding Easter eggs.

A barrier of viburnum and pines renders the golf course invisible from our property. The plants muffle the curses of frustrated golfers, but the jubilant cry, "A hole in one!" I have clearly heard twice in the three summers we've dwelt here.

As for shouts of "Fore!" I am fond of saying that "we can't hear the 'Fores' for the trees."

The county also owns a grassy meadow adjoining our property. It is not part of the golf course, merely a wide open area along the section of the course that borders our street. Driving past our house, anyone would assume that the meadow was part of our property. I've planted tall grasses and several trees on it, and I share the responsibility, with the park's grounds crew, of keeping it mowed.

Ray, the old-timer who mows the park's portion of that meadow, has become a friend. He is "an old guy who can still hack it," and I love to hear about his backpacking with his grandchildren or kayaking with his wife. He has keen gray eyes, a little gray mustache, and eyebrows to match. When we spy one another, we drop what we're doing and have what folks back home in Richland County term "a good chin-wag." Leaning on either side of the green picket fence that separates my own garden from the meadow, Ray and I recount our adventures and exchange "old husbands' tales."

One day I told Ray the story of my discovery of the Blue Rock, in much the same words I used in Chapter One of this book. He was intrigued, as I knew he would be. I opened the gate in the picket fence and we ambled over to the Blue Rock, at the center of the far side of the lower garden, up against the fence, just a few yards from the edge of the golf course. It's from there that Jo and I toss the golf balls we find, through the viburnum and back onto the golf course.

Ray squatted down next to the Blue Rock and studied it earnestly for a good while. Then he did something no other Blue Rock initiate had thought to do. He rolled it over to inspect its underside.

"The bottom is flat!" he observed. "Almost perfectly flat. You don't generally find a flat-bottomed rock. Which makes me think that this is not rock at all. It's concrete. It's been crudely piled up and it cured while lying on a flat surface."

"But how do you explain the blueness of it?"

"Epoxy paint. Like the kind they use to seal a concrete garage floor. You can do it yourself for cheap, or you can hire professionals who will sand your garage floor and then cover it with epoxy paint to seal it up good."

"Does epoxy paint come in colors?"

"Sure. Any color you want."

"Even a sort of quartz-looking blue like this? with striations?"

"Well, yes, though getting those white striations just right would take some doing."

"But who would fashion such a thing out of concrete, coat it with blue epoxy paint and then lug it so far into the woods? And why?"

We both pondered this for a while in silence.

Then Ray conjectured, "Maybe someone fabricated the rock out of concrete right there in the woods. They'd have had to lug in a bag of concrete mix, a five-gallon jerry can of water, and a wheelbarrow to mix it in, but it would be way easier to make the thing right there on the spot as opposed to making it somewhere else and then dragging it there."

"That makes sense," I said.

Ray warmed to his own idea. "Then they'd have to come back, well, maybe a hundred times, to apply a hundred coats of blue epoxy paint. They'd have to let each coat dry for a day before applying the next coat, but if a person was persistent, it could be done. A hundred layers of epoxy paint would explain the transparency of the blue in some places on the rock."

"But who would do such a ridiculous thing?" I still wanted to know. "And why?"

I thought about it quite a lot in the days that followed.

Then it hit me. Cy Gatton would do such a thing. Why hadn't I thought of him before? As to his motivations, I bet I could make a pretty good guess.

Who was Cy Gatton?

In answer, I'll paraphrase the opening of *The Adventures of Huckleberry Finn*:

> You don't know about Cy Gatton, without you have read a book by the name of *Ripsnorting Whoppers: Humor from America's Heartland*; but that ain't no matter. That book was made by Mr. Rick Sowash and he told the truth, mainly. There was things which he stretched, but mainly he told the truth.

That book begins:

> Nearly two centuries ago, a shabby little man by the name of John Chapman made his way into the wilderness of north-central Ohio. He left in his wake a legacy of apple trees and stories. Both took root, and today every schoolchild has heard of Johnny Appleseed ... an historic figure cloaked in myths.

Just eighteen years after the pioneer nurseryman died, Cyrus Miller Gatton was born in the same Richland County that Johnny Appleseed knew so well. Both Johnny and Cy were outdoorsmen wise in the ways of nature. Both were ragged in appearance, yet, in what might appear to us to be a paradox, both "businessmen" were widely admired and even loved. And both Johnny and Cy are linked to that American tradition of humor called the tall tale.

Johnny Appleseed stuck to the planting of trees, letting others tell the stories, but Cy Gatton did both. For much of his life, Cy was busy raising trees and spinning tales, "ripsnorting whoppers" about Richland County and its amazing soil, weather and creatures. They were outrageous "stretchers" that would make his listeners gasp in amazement and then roar with laughter.

Cy Gatton (1863-1938) lived his whole life on the family farm on the Clear Fork River that flows through north-central Ohio. That area, lying halfway between Columbus and Cleveland, is a gently rolling countryside where five little rivers come together like the fingers on a hand to form the Mohican. They are the Black Fork, the Rocky Fork, the Muddy Fork, the Cedar Fork, and Cy Gatton's beloved Clear Fork, all forks of one river that has given its name to the area, sometimes called "the Mohican Country."

The great-grandson of Isaac Gatton, one of the earliest settlers of Richland County, Cy came of age during the prosperous decades following the Civil War. It was a time when the richest man around was still, generally, the farmer, and story-telling was the dominant form of rural entertainment.

Like Johnny Appleseed, Cy planted trees. But while Johnny's footloose ways carried him from Pennsylvania to Indiana, Cy stayed in one place, raising a family and growing a nursery business. His business, now called the Wade & Gatton Nursery, is still going strong, and it's still in the family.

We don't know when Cy started telling whoppers, but probably it was pretty early on. Most of his stories were traditional favorites, but what made them different was the way he made himself the central figure in them, creating a character that is Ohio's answer to Paul Bunyan, Pecos Bill, Davy Crockett and Mike Fink.

Cy's first audiences were most likely his family, friends and neighbors. Then, in the 1890s, Cy developed "Gatton Rocks." This was a resort named for the sixty-foot, pine-peppered rock formations that loom above the Clear Fork River as it passes through the Gatton farm. Cy offered vacationers cottages for rent, swimming in the Clear Fork, and even a tennis court. People came down from Mansfield and Cleveland and up from

Newark and Columbus. The train even made a whistle stop at "Gatton Rocks."

The vacationers came for the ageless pleasures of summer: picnics, swimming and taking in the scenery. Mostly, though, they came because of Cy Gatton himself. He was "such a character," a perpetrator of pranks and practical jokes. He was full of fun and bursting with stories about all the amazing things that happened on that remarkable property of his.

Cy especially liked telling about the preposterous goings-on back in the woods up behind his big house where the soil was so fertile that he was afraid to plant anything back there until one day ...

... but you'll have to read my book, *Ripsnorting Whoppers*, if you want that story and many others.

To get back to the Blue Rock, my thoughts went to Cy when I remembered of one of his stories that I discovered too late to be included in *Ripsnorting Whoppers*.

One summer evening Cy Gatton went out to his barnyard. He pushed his hands under his belt, pursed his lips and sniffed the cool, sweet air though his big, bushy walrus mustache. He was watching the lightning bugs rise out of the grass, little yellow blinks in the half-darkness. His old wrinkly face broke out in a big wrinkly smile. He loved lightning bugs. So pretty. You don't think of them all winter long, and then one summer evening, there they are.

Then he saw that he wasn't the only one watching the lightning bugs. His favorite laying-hen was watching them, too, strange to tell.

Then he saw that she wasn't just watching them. She was chasing them!

Then he saw that she wasn't just chasing them. She was eating them!

Now, Cy had never heard of a chicken eating lightning bugs. It was the most unheard-of thing he'd ever heard of. Suddenly it came to him that this chicken might be on to a good thing. "If this chicken'll eat lightning bugs," he reasoned, "it'll save us money on chicken feed! Lightning bugs are free!"

He yelled to his kids. "C'mon out and catch some lightning bugs!" Earl and Nell Gatton exploded out of the house and ran round the barnyard, catching the lightning bugs in glass jars. Then they poured all the lightning bugs they had caught into a big bowl.

There must have been a hundred lightning bugs in that bowl, easy. They set it down in front of the chicken. She pecked-up and swallowed down every last one of them.

Then she turned and went back to her nest in the chicken coop. Cy and the kids went inside the Gatton farmhouse and ate supper. Cy told a few tall tales to the kids, and then the family all went to bed.

In the middle of the night, Cy woke up, sudden-like. What had awakened him? He was worrying about that chicken. Would she be all right? Maybe they shouldn't have given her so many lightning bugs to eat.

Cy got out of bed and went to the window. He pulled aside the curtain. A few stars peeked through the leaves of the great sycamores around Cy's house.

Cy looked across the pitch-black barnyard. In the starlight he could just make out the chicken coop. He half-thought he might see a weird yellow glow coming out of that coop. But everything seemed normal.

Still, Cy was worried. He pulled on his pants, went downstairs and outside. The dusty ground felt soft and cool under his bare feet as he crossed the barnyard. He slowly pushed open the door of the chicken coop and the rusty hinges made their usual high-pitched, scraping sound.

There was the chicken, sitting on her nest. He half-thought he might see a weird yellow glow coming out of her eyes. But everything still seemed okay.

"Well," he said, "I guess I've come out here for nothin'."

Then he supposed he might as well look in her nest, the way he did first thing every morning. That's what people do on a farm, first thing. They look in the hen's nest.

He shooshed her aside, just the way he did every morning, not thinking anything about it. He looked in her nest. And that was when he come to find that the chicken, after eating all those lightning bugs, had laid …

A DOZEN ELECTRIC LIGHT BULBS!

Cy's reputation as a storyteller spread. As he reached his fifties, he found himself in demand as a professional humorous speaker, telling his stories at banquets and picnics throughout north-central Ohio.

By the mid-1930s, near the end of his life, Cy's mastery of the tall tale brought him, briefly, to national attention. Lowell Thomas, a fellow Ohioan and the most famous news commentator of his day, heard Cy entertain a banquet audience and was captivated. Later, in a nationally heard radio broadcast, Thomas presented Cy with a certificate of membership in an exclusive organization the newscaster had founded, "The Tall Story Club of New York." The certificate is delightfully worded; I'll quote it in full.

> Know all men by these presents that it is my tall privilege to give high testimony that Cy Gatton, who tells them tall, with a lofty sacrifice of veracity, has proven his altitudinous devotion to The Great American Whopper, and is hereby elevated to the rank of Exalted Ananias of the Tall Story Club.

It was the high point of Cy's long career, and if he had lived another ten years, Ohio might have been able to claim a nationally celebrated folk hero all its own – a kind of Mark Twain, Will Rogers and Garrison Keillor rolled into one uniquely Buckeye character.

Cy was greatly rejoiced by the honor and attention Lowell Thomas had lavished upon him. Still, for Cy and for millions of his fellow Americans, times were tough. The Great Depression lay heavily upon the land. The nursery business dried up and the side income Cy earned from speaking at banquets and picnics was not huge. Too, he always shared his stories free of charge for Scouts, 4-H'ers and church groups.

But Cy's Gatton Rocks resort was off the beaten path, and visitors were few in number. Something more was needed to draw the visitors who would rent cottages and buy hardtack, beans and rice in Cy's modest store. Swimming in the Clear Fork, climbing the cliffs, and being entertained by Cy's storytelling were not enough to pull in crowds. Cy needed to create an "Attraction."

But what? Ohio's Office of Tourism has wrestled with this problem for decades. For all its blessings, the Buckeye State has little to compare with the best of its rivals. There is no Grand Canyon, no Niagara Falls, no Mammoth Cave, no Gettsyburg Battlefield, no Statue of Liberty. Lake Erie is fine and dandy, but it is the least exciting of the five Great Lakes. The Ohio River is a big strong river, but it gets only Honorable Mention when compared with the Mississippi, the Missouri, the Colorado or the scenic Snake.

We have the famous and justly celebrated Serpent Mound, true. Cy thought of constructing an animal effigy mound on the flood plain along the Clear Fork that could rival it. Maybe a mound in the shape of a giant squirrel, twice as large as the Serpent Mound. He envisioned billboards ornamenting highways across the state: "See the Great Squirrel Mound at Gatton Rocks." He sketched plans for it but bringing that particular dream to reality would require a dozen bulldozers and a dozen men to operate them. It was beyond his means.

He pondered the tourist attractions that already existed in Ohio. The amusement park at Cedar Point seemed to be getting by, despite the Depression. But no research was required to know that building an amusement park at Gatton Rocks would be even more costly than building the Great Squirrel Mound.

There was also "The Blue Hole." In the 1930s all Ohioans had seen the hundreds of billboards that beckoned, "See the Mysterious Blue Hole in Castalia, Ohio." When I was growing up in Mansfield in the 1950s, those billboards were still a common sight, right along with Burma-Shave signs, though by that time they were looking pretty ragged with age. Thousands of Ohioans made a day of it, visiting the Blue Hole and Cheesehaven, then swimming and picnicking at East Harbor.

One Saturday in May of 1937, Cy made the sixty-five-mile trip with his wife Etta Pearl, their kids and grandkids in tow, all the way up to Castalia. He paid the admission fee for the lot of them, and they immediately went to view the purported wonder. To Cy's surprise and his family's disappointment, the Blue Hole didn't amount to much. A circular pond is all it was, about seventy-five feet across. It was pretty enough, the water being a vibrant blue hue (maybe, Cy thought, with the help of a gallon or two of blue food coloring being tossed in every couple of days).

The only thing that was "mysterious" about it was the claim that it was bottomless. The tour guide told the gaping crowds that all attempts to plumb the depths of the Blue Hole had been in vain, that it seemed to have no bottom; that it had been designated as one of the Seven Enigmas of the Natural World. (The other six were not identified.) This fired the imaginations of the gullible with visions of the places Jules Verne had described in his *Journey to the Center of the Earth*. Who knew what might be hidden in the supposedly unfathomable depths of the Blue Hole?

All in all, it was a nice enough day trip for a family from Bellville, but nothing more. Still, Cy was impressed with the concept. He got to talking with the manager, who told him that the Blue Hole was drawing 165,000 visitors annually, despite the Depression. The depth of the Blue Hole may have been in dispute, but there was no doubt about its success as a tourist attraction.

It set Cy to thinking. He had to create something from scratch, something blue and, in one way or another, "mysterious."

He considered, deeply, perhaps for the first time, the sources of his own talents. Where had his famous "gift of gab" come from? Most people said they were terrified of getting up in front of an audience, but Cy had always thrived on it. Stage fright had never come upon him.

All those stories that had come to him, all those tall tales — What had been their source? Into what treasury had he been somehow able to dip? He could no more explain the origins of his stories than the tour guides at the Blue Hole could explain the Delphian depths of that otherwise-undistinguished little body of water.

Then he remembered something a little red-haired fellow had said to him after one of his speeches at a picnic. "Mr. Gatton," he had said, in a distinctive Irish accent, "that was a hoot and a roar. 'Tis sure you must've kissed the Blarney Stone."

The what? Cy had let it pass at the time, but now he became curious. What had the fellow meant? What was this Blarney Stone? He consulted Miss Newsbickle, the reference librarian who ran the tiny Bellville Public Library.

The Blarney Stone, he learned, is a block of limestone that is part of the battlements of Blarney Castle in Ireland. The legend about the stone holds that people who kiss the stone find themselves, afterwards and always, endowed with the ability to deceive without offending or doing harm.

"Heck," thought Cy. "I've been doing that all my life."

Cy had never been to Ireland – or much of anywhere beyond north-central Ohio – so he could certainly not claim to have kissed the original Blarney Stone or any other stone he could remember.

But what if there was another Blarney Stone, an American Blarney Stone, somewhere deep in the woods behind his farm and nursery? By a modest stretch of credulity, he could claim that he had been kissing the stone regularly ever since he was a boy and that, mysteriously, the experience seemed to have gifted him with his spectacular talents as a storyteller.

It was as good an explanation as any other, and he could see no harm in such an assertion, just as there had been no harm in any other of those tall tales he had told over the years. It would be understood as just another Cy Gatton story. People would be delighted. They always were.

One thing, though. It had to be blue. What would the Blue Hole be, Cy thought, if it weren't blue? What would the billboards say – "See the Mysterious Hole in Castalia, Ohio"? That would be ridiculous. But a hole that is both mysterious and blue, well, that's a thing to behold.

Thus was born one of Cy's last great ideas, The Blue Blarney Stone. He couldn't afford to rent space on billboards, but he and his son Earl could build one easily enough, out along State Route 97, where it came up against the edge of his property. They could paint it, too. A white background with big blue letters: "Kiss the Mysterious Blue Blarney Stone at Gatton Rocks."

He would charge visitor a dime and serve as their tour guide, leading them back in the woods and telling them a few of his best tall tales along the way. And when they arrived, he would arrange them in a circle around the Blue Blarney Stone, talk about it a bit, and invite them all to plant a smacker on it.

All he needed was a blue rock. But it couldn't just be sky blue, like the ordinary paint that anybody could buy. It had to induce wonder. The blue had to be … what words could adequately describe his vision of it? … radiant, iridescent, luminous, phosphorescent, lustrous, and translucent.

Come July, he went up to the Sherwin Williams shop in Mansfield and told the resident paint expert there that he needed to acquire, for reasons he was not at liberty to share, a bucket of extraordinary blue paint. No ordinary shade of blue would serve, he explained. The effect he was after must be radiant, iridescent, luminous, phosphorescent, lustrous, and translucent.

"What you want," the fellow told him confidently, "is epoxy paint. But one or two coats won't do the trick. What you'll need to do is apply dozens, even hundreds of coats, letting each one dry before you paint on the next one, so that you get this layered, almost transparent effect. And you're gonna go through a lot of brushes, I'll tell you right now."

Cy went home with a bucket of blue epoxy paint and a dozen brushes.

Now he needed a rock. But just as no ordinary shade of blue would serve, so, too, no ordinary rock would do. It had to be something special, something unique, something unlike any of the other rocks that lay on the forest floor where the glaciers had left them.

He would have to make it from scratch, out of concrete. At first, he thought that it should be big, even huge. Taller than a man and just as wide. But if he made something like that in his barn, how would he transport it back into the woods? He'd have to make the thing on the spot at a location of his own choosing in the deepest part of the woods.

He loaded his wheelbarrow with a bag of concrete mix and a five-gallon jerry can of water and made his way into the woods. He was a little dismayed at how quickly he found himself short of breath. He stopped and rested for a bit, and when his breathing slowed down to normal, he proceeded. He had to stop several times along the way, but finally he was content that he had arrived in the center of the forest.

For a week, Cy returned every day, huffing and puffing, arriving at last, mixing a little more concrete and adding it to the growing mass. He took pains to make it uneven and odd-looking, smooth in some places, rough in others. When he was satisfied with the shape and size of it – considerably smaller than he had originally conceived, but still almost too heavy for one man to oomph – he spent an entire day using a hand drill to pierce it with holes in random places, changing the drill bit every time so that no two holes would have the same diameter.

Then, when the last layer of concrete had cured, he returned to apply blue epoxy paint. Day after day, he returned. The brushes could not be cleaned and had to be thrown away after a single use, which was painful for Cy. He sent his son Earl up to Sherwin Williams to buy twenty-five more and, when those were used up, twenty-five more.

September came and went. The leaves were turning yellow, scarlet, purple and orange. The ferns were a havoc of pale gold. The Blue Blarney Stone was coming along. Cy reflected that, except for the sky and the water, blue was a color rarely seen in nature. There were bluebirds, blue robin's eggs, blueberries, blue shadows on the snow and a few semi-precious blue stones; but that was about it. There were no blue mammals, frogs, turtles, snakes or fish. There are bluegills but only their gills are blue – and that, not very. A few salamanders, maybe. We talk about "a blue moon" when the moon is never blue. Nature was mostly green, gray and brown. Cy mused. It seemed like there was an opening there for a new tall tale, maybe one for the ages.

Etta Pearl, noticing Cy's shortness of breath when he climbed the stairs to their bedroom, worried about him. She insisted that he see "the Doc" in Bellville. When the Doc told him his heart was wearing out, he laughed, "Then I guess the only thing is for me to get a new one."

Meanwhile his creation of the Blue Blarney Stone was pleasing him immensely. He was deeply excited. He thought that, when it was finished, he would build seating for the visitors, setting logs on the ground with two-by-eight boards spanning them, like the seating around the Scout campfires at which he had often told stories.

But he never got that far. As October of 1938 came to an end, so did Cy's efforts to realize his vision. Coming back from the woods one day, he felt a sort of cramp in his chest. He barely managed to climb the steps behind his house, and the floor of the back porch seemed to be pitching and tossing like a canoe in the rapids of the Clear Fork. He entered the kitchen. To steady himself, he grasped the kitchen table with both hands. He fell. When Etta Pearl found him lying there and touched him, she knew that he was gone.

*   *   *

Cy was a real person, and the stories he left behind, some more far-fetched than this one, are lovely antiques that we can still enjoy. I collected them by perusing old newspaper articles and interviewing his grandchildren, who were themselves elderly when I met with them in the late 1970s. His stories connect us with the past with a depth of feeling that few history books can provide.

But their fascination for modern listeners goes still deeper, touching the mystic in all of us. At the heart of each of Cy's stories there is An Unanswerable Question. Why are there limits on anything? What determines the maximum speed at which a plant can grow? Why can't a catfish be trained to live outside the water? Why can the fastest dog run only so fast and no faster? Since Time and Space are limitless – or at least inconceivably long and vast – why must lives – and books – have beginnings and endings? Why can't they just go on and on?

Such questions are usually asked only by children and philosophers, perhaps by an exceptional scientist. Cy didn't try to answer them. What fascinated Cy was the challenge of merely posing these questions in the guise of tall tales, stories so vividly conceived and delightfully told that they "deceive without offending," subtly enticing people to ponder The Great Imponderables … all the while diverting, entertaining, and inspiring both the teller and the told.

12

Another Beginning

THERE WAS A MAN who lived in a village near a dark forest.

The village was Bellville, Ohio.

One day, walking in the forest, the man came upon something surprising and mysterious: a blue rock.

How did it get there? What sort of rock was it? What did its presence in the forest mean? Who could tell its story?

The man had to possess it.

A friend helped him transport the blue rock to his home. It became, for him, "The Blue Rock." Years later, when he sold his house and moved, he took the Blue Rock with him. All through his long life, wherever he lived, the Blue Rock graced his garden.

When he showed the Blue Rock to friends, many offered ideas as to its origins and various explanations of how it came to rest in the dark forest near Bellville. Their imaginative accounts delighted him.

He learned that the great English poet Gerard Manley Hopkins had been fascinated by mineralogy as a boy. Later the poet-to-be realized that what fascinated him was not the chemistry, structure, or properties of the minerals, nor the accounts of their origins, nor their classification, geographical distribution, or utilization. What fascinated the poet-to-be were their beautiful names.

This anecdote spoke to the man. The value of the Blue Rock was not its chemical makeup. What rendered it a thing of value to him was its beauty and mystery. The beautiful and, to him, mysterious names of the various blue minerals he read about expressed that notion. He sought out the names of blue gems and kept a list of those with the most beautiful, curious, and mysterious-sounding names.

Amazonite
Apatite
Azurite
Celestine
Chalcedony
Hawk's eye
Lapis lazuli
Moonstone
Opal
Sapphire
Sillimanite
Spinel
Topaz
Tourmaline

Serene in the knowledge that he himself was a "silly man," he smiled when he thought of the mineral "Sillimanite."

The man contacted experts, sending them photos and descriptions of the Blue Rock.

One wrote, "It appears to be an aggregate of some sort. The conchoidal fracture looks like it could be a variety of flint which is abundant in Ohio." The man did not believe it was flint. He had seen plenty of flint and none of it resembled the Blue Rock.

When he looked up "conchoidal fracture" he found it described as "a smoothly curving fracture of fine-grained materials characteristic of glass and other materials having no crystalline structure." That seemed to validate the suggestion of one of his friends that the Blue Rock was a by-product of the manufacture of fine glassware.

The wittiest response was from an expert who suggested that the stone was Apatite, and that the Blue Rock had been left in the woods because "someone had lost his Apatite."

A more imaginative but less helpful expert sent him an account of a discovery made in Sierra Leone by an Italian explorer named Pitoni. He was looking for signs of the presence of diamonds in an area known as Kono when he met a local chieftain who, to Pitoni's amazement, scraped away a few inches of topsoil to reveal a blue stone with mysterious white lines on its surface.

The chief recounted a legend about a rebellion of angels who, after being expelled from Heaven, fell to the earth, bringing thousands of stars with them as well as a bevy of blue rocks. The stars were scattered in the region and accounted for the diamonds discovered there as well as the occasional blue rock.

Pitoni returned to Italy with his blue rock and consulted geologists, mineralogists, and gemologists. Some, upon examining Pitoni's blue rock, noted that over the years a few similar blue rocks had appeared elsewhere, but so rarely that they might not have originated on earth. Some said that these "Sky Stones," as the rocks came to be called, offered evidence of ancient alien visits or advanced civilizations now lost to history. The man thought this kind of theorizing was ridiculous and steered clear of the self-styled experts who propounded such stuff.

The man lived a long life, enjoyed a colorful and flourishing career, was blessed with good health and a loving family. He was doubly blessed with a circle of highly intelligent, creative, and imaginative friends to whom he never tired of showing the Blue Rock, asking them to make their best guesses as to its provenance. In so doing he gathered many stories, which he told in turn to other friends who admired the Blue Rock over the years.

When he was well stricken in years, his sharing of these stories became the elderly gentleman's supereminent whim. His mind, somewhat oblivious of the present and thus beyond "the rebuffs of surprise or the vicissitudes of change," was chiefly engaged in tracing the backward arc of an eventful life, pondering what it had all meant. At last, still in the full vigor of life, he passed gently in his sleep.

Honoring his wishes, his family hired an airplane and directed the pilot to fly over southern Richland County, asking him to alert them when the craft was above the largest forested area between Bellville and Butler.

They had brought the man's ashes as well as the blue rock he had discovered in the area many years before. It was heavy but oomphable. When the moment was right, they made their last farewells and dispersed his dust out the airplane's door, followed by the blue rock.

The dust instantly vanished into the ether. The rock plummeted and landed with a thud unheard by human ears. And there it lay.

*   *   *

A short time later, the blue rock was discovered anew by another man who lived in a village near a dark forest. I am that man.

Made in the USA
Monee, IL
27 October 2021